NEW WRITINGS IN S-F is a successful *new* departure in the science fiction field, bringing to lovers of the *genre*, new stories specially written for the series by well-known as well as new authors. Its presentation exclusively in volume form is the next step forward in expanding the S-F short story from the limitations it has suffered in magazine publication during the past thirty years and introduces international authors writing for a far wider audience than ever before. This twelfth volume includes stories by James White, M. John Harrison, John Rankine, David Rome, Arthur Sellings and Colin Kapp.

NEW WRITINGS IN S-F
(12)

Edited by
JOHN CARNELL

LONDON: DENNIS DOBSON

All the characters in this book are fictitious
and any resemblance to actual persons,
living or dead, is purely coincidental.

First published in Great Britain in 1968 by Dobson Books Ltd.,
80 Kensington Church Street, London W.8

SBN 234 77968 3

Printed in Great Britain by Richard Clay (The Chaucer Press), Ltd.,
Bungay, Suffolk

CONTENTS

FOREWORD

by

JOHN CARNELL

SEVERAL years ago I predicted in a magazine editorial that the 1960s would see some sweeping changes in the general presentation of ideas in science-fiction stories and that the *genre* might well take some unexpected twists and turns. In fact, there was little magic in my crystal gazing because the whole character of S-F story-telling apparently follows very closely to the 11-year sun-spot cycle and since the inception of magazine short-story publication in the mid-20s there have been four major changes of style. A fifth has been developing during this present decade.

The two significant current changes evolved separately on either side of the Atlantic and will obviously influence the *genre* for many years to come, just as the secret agent influenced the thriller field. In the U.K. the most notable approach to S-F writing was produced by J. G. Ballard in his short stories and novels, using thought complexes of story-telling which he defined as "inner space" in an article as far back as May 1962. Practising what he personally advocated, Mr. Ballard has brought a new concept to the hitherto hide-bound fiction of interplanetary travel by ignoring it and placing his plots on Earth in meta-physical settings.

To quote from his article, "I would like to see more psycho-literary ideas, more meta-biological and meta-chemical concepts, private time-systems, synthetic psychologies and space-times, more of the remote, sombre half-worlds one glimpses in paintings of schizophrenics, all in all a complete speculative poetry and fantasy of science." In his own works, Mr. Ballard produces an abstract form of S-F writing in keeping with present-day trends. It isn't easy to write and demands a high literary standard to make it effective. A good example of his influence is shown in new author M. John Harrison's story "Visions of Monad", in this volume.

Meanwhile, across the Atlantic, a completely different facet of the S-F story suddenly developed—a form I have called "mediaeval futurism". Future technologies, often on other planets, but with heavy overtones of the Middle Ages feudal systems as the governing bodies. One of the earliest isolated examples of this style was L. Sprague de Camp's satire *Divide and Rule*, written in 1939, but the general idea lay fallow (except for other de Camp stories) until 1960 when Poul Anderson wrote *The High Crusade*. Since then the "mediaeval futurism" novel has been developed by a succession of American authors, in particular Jack Vance with his *The Dragon Masters* and Keith Laumer with his "Worlds of the Imperium" series.

The closest example we have in this volume is Colin Kapp's radical departure from his normal technique in "The Cloudbuilders", but a much better example was Vincent King's novelette, "The Wall to End the World" in No. 11.

Despite the new variations, however, the older established middle-of-the-road stories are just as popular and the rest of the stories in this volume are first-class examples of the many variations on a theme or themes. James White's second "Sector General" novelette for this series, "Vertigo", contains all the overtones of a good science-fiction story in an alien setting, while the strong characterisation and story-telling in both Arthur Sellings' "The Last Time Around" and David Rome's "They Shall Reap" could only be told in their

8

present style. There is nothing out of place in John Rankine's space-mystery, "Worm in the Bud", either.

Whatever the changing facets may be in the S-F writing field, you can be sure that *New Writings In S-F* will be keeping up with them, now and in the future.

JOHN CARNELL

August 1967.

VERTIGO

by

JAMES WHITE

Continuing the new series of Sector Twelve General Hospital stories, which commenced in New Writings In S-F 7 with "Invader", Doctors Conway and Prilicla and the staff of the vast hospital in space are faced with saving the life of a first astronaut in space. However, both the patient and his home planet were very strange indeed.

VERTIGO

ONE

AFTER that one brief and hectic touch-down when the clearing they had chosen as a landing area had suddenly opened an enormous mouth and tried to swallow them, the Survey and Cultural Contact vessel *Descartes* had returned to continue its study of Meatball from orbit.

Christened Meatball because Galactic Survey Reference NT117/136/5 was verbally cumbersome and because *Descartes'* Captain had steadfastly refused the honour of having such an odd and distasteful place named after him, the planet had to be seen to be believed. Its oceans were a thick, living soup, its inland seas and lakes a turgid, heaving stew and its land masses, or what on a normal planet would correspond to a land surface, were a multi-layer carpet of slow-moving animal life.

In many places there were mineral outcroppings and areas of rocky soil which supported vegetable life and other forms of vegetation grew in the water or rooted themselves temporarily on the "land" surface, their chief purpose being the assimilation of wastes. But generally the planet was covered by a thick layer of animal life which in some areas was several miles deep. This organic layer was subdivided into strata which crawled and slipped and fought their way through each other to gain access to necessary top-surface vegetation or subsurface minerals, or simply to choke off and cannibalise each other. In the course of this slow, gargantuan conflict these living geologic strata heaved themselves into hills and valleys, altering the shape of lakes and coastlines and changing the topography of the planet from week to week.

The data gathered by *Descartes* before and during the landing attempt led to a great deal of theorising and dis-'cussion.

It was generally agreed that if the planet possessed intelligent life it should take two forms. The first type would be large—one of the tremendous living carpets which could anchor itself to the underlying rock or soil for mineral supplies and also push extensions towards the surface for the purpose of breathing, ingestion and the disposal of wastes. It should also possess a means of defence around its perimeter to keep less intelligent strata from insinuating themselves between it and the ground below or from slipping over it and cutting it off from the surface water, food and air. They were assuming, of course, that real intelligence in a massive organism would require a permanent base from which to develop.

The second possibility might be a very small life-form. It should be smooth-skinned and flexible to enable it to slip between the intersurfaces of the strata animals on its way to and from the surface, and it should be able to withstand considerable pressure and to move fast enough to escape the ingestive processes of the larger types whose movements and metabolism would be relatively slow. At the same time this second type should be large enough to live off the smaller animal and vegetable matter of the seas and non-living land surfaces and their fixed base, if they needed one, might be a cave or tunnel system in the underlying rock.

Specimens of the first type were spread across the planetary surface for all to see, but they showed no indications of being intelligent, and traces of the second type were still being formed.

It was perhaps inevitable that when the long awaited indication of intelligent life at last appeared the majority of the ship's observers were looking somewhere else, that it did not appear in the batteries of telescopes that were being trained on the surface or on the still and cine films being taken by *Descartes'* planetary probes, but on the vessel's close-approach radar screens.

Close in time but at a point distant in space, in the office of the Chief Psychologist of Sector Twelve General Hospital, the world of Meatball and its inhabitants were likewise the subject of a serious and single-minded discussion. Present were Major O'Mara the chief psychologist, Senior Physicians Mannen, Prilicla and Conway, and a small, metallic ... *something* ... which squirmed and quivered and changed its shape from moment to moment.

A few seconds earlier it had been an elaborately decorated ash-tray and before that a rather lobsided bust of Shakespeare but now, because more than one person was thinking at it simultaneously, it resembled a small, solidified nightmare.

"Maybe we shouldn't do this," said Mannen suddenly. "We may be inflicting grave psychological damage, a form of schizophrenia perhaps..."

"I'm not the psychologist," said Conway, laughing, "but I find the idea of a psychotic monkey-wrench difficult to accept..."

"I am, and I refuse to commit myself," said O'Mara drily. He went on, "But we are getting away from the point of this discussion, which is to discover a means of obtaining more, many more, of these ... these ..." He broke off, breathed heavily through his nose and continued, "Normally I am not a covetous man, but when you consider all the things we could *do* with them, of what the Hospital could do with just ten of them, or even five..."

Sector General was a multi-environmental hospital, a tremendous, complex fabrication of metal which hung in space like a man-made moon. Inside its three hundred and eighty-four levels were reproduced the environments of all the intelligent life-forms known to the Galactic Federation, a biological spectrum ranging from the ultra-frigid methane species through the more normal oxygen- and chlorine-breathing types up to the exotic beings who existed by the direct conversion of hard radiation. In addition to the patients, whose number and physiological classification was a constant variable, there was a medical and maintenance staff which was composed of sixty-odd differing life-forms with sixty different sets of mannerisms, body odours and ways of looking at life.

The medical staff of Sector General was an extremely able, dedicated, but not always serious group of people who were fanatically tolerant of all forms of intelligent life—had this not been so they could never have served in a multi-environment hospital in the first place. They prided themselves that no case was too big, too small or too hopeless, and their professional reputation and facilities were second to none. But until now their facilities had not included that surgeon's wish-fulfillment dream come true, an instrument which would take any desired shape and degree of sharpness, an all-purpose surgical tool which was subject to the user's mental as well as manual control.

"... But we have only one of the things!" O'Mara continued vehemently. "We need more! This one found its way—or was directed, rather—on board *Descartes* during that momentary landing on Meatball. If we were doing the right thing we would put it back where we found it—obviously it is of enormous value. This means that we will have to buy them or conduct some form of trade for them. But to do so we must first be able to communicate with the owners."

He glanced at the three doctors in turn, then went on sardonically, "One hesitates to mention such sordid commercial matters to pure-minded, dedicated medical men like yourselves, but I must do so if only to explain why, when *Descartes* eventually makes contact with the beings who own these tools, I want you three to head the team which will investigate the medical situation on Meatball.

"Our interest will not be entirely commercial, of course," he added quickly, "but it seems to me that if we have to go in for the practice of barter and exchange, the only thing we have to trade is our medical knowledge and services . . ."

In *Descartes'* control-room the Captain jabbed a button on his console and said sharply, "Communications . . .?"

"We have it, sir," came the reply. "A telescope locked on to the radar bearing—the image is on your repeater screen Five. It is a two- or three-stage chemically fuelled vehicle with the second stage still firing. This means we will be able to reconstruct its flight path and pinpoint the launch area with fair accuracy. It is emitting complex patterns of radio frequency radiation indicative of high-speed telemetry channels. The second stage has just cut out and is falling away. The third stage, if it is a third stage, has not ignited . . . It's in trouble!"

The alien spacecraft, a slim, shining cylinder pointed at one end and thickened and blunt at the other, had begun to tumble. Slowly at first but with steadily increasing speed it swung and whirled end over end.

"Ordnance?" asked the Captain.

"Apart from the tumbling action," said a slower, more precise voice, "the vessel seems to have been inserted into a very neat circular orbit. It is most unlikely that this orbit was taken up by accident. The lack of sophistication relative, that is—in the vehicle's design and the fact that its nearest approach to us will be a little under two hundred miles all point to the conclusion that it is either an artificial satellite or a manned orbiting vehicle rather than a missile directed at this ship.

"If it is manned," the voice added with more feeling, "the crew must be in serious trouble . . ."

"Yes," said the Captain, who treated words like nuggets of some rare and precious metal. He went on, "Astrogation, prepare intersecting and matching orbits, please. Power Room, stand by."

As the tremendous bulk of *Descartes* closed with the tiny alien craft it became apparent that, as well as tumbling dizzily end over end, the other vessel was leaking. The rapid spin made it impossible to say with certainty whether it was a fuel leak from the unfired third stage or air escaping from the command module if it was, in fact, a manned vehicle.

The obvious procedure was to check the spin with tractor beams as gently as possible so as to avoid straining the hull structure, then de-fuel the unfired third stage to remove the fire hazard before bringing the craft alongside. If the vessel was manned and the leak was of air rather than fuel, it could then be taken into *Descartes'* cargo hold where rescue and first contact proceedings would be possible—at leisure since Meatball's air was suited to human beings and the reverse, presumably, also held true.

It was expected to be a fairly simple rescue operation, at first . . .

"Tractor stations Six and Seven, sir. The alien spacecraft won't stay put. We've slowed it to a stop three times and each time it applies steering thrust and recommences spinning. For some reason it is deliberately fighting our efforts to bring it to rest. The speed and quality of the reaction suggests direction by an on-the-spot intelligence. We can apply more force, but only at the risk of damaging the vessel's hull—it is incredibly fragile by present-day standards, sir."

"I suggest using all necessary force to immediately check the spin, opening its tanks and jettisoning all fuel into space then whisking it into the cargo hold. With normal air pressure around it again there will be no danger to the crew and we will have time to . . ."

"Astrogation, here. Negative to that, I'm afraid, sir. Our computation shows that the vessel took off from the sea— more accurately, from beneath the sea, because there is no visible evidence of floating gantries or other launch facilities in the area. We can reproduce Meatball air because it is virtually the same as our own, but not that animal and vegetable soup they use for water, and all the indications point towards the crew being water-breathers."

For a few seconds the Captain did not reply. He was thinking about the alien crew member or members and their reasons for behaving as they were doing. Whether the reason was technical, physiological, psychological or simply alien was, however, of secondary importance. The main thing was to render assistance as quickly as possible.

If his own ship could not aid the other vessel directly it could, in a matter of days, take it to a place which possessed all the necessary facilities for doing so. Transportation itself posed only a minor problem—the spinning vehicle could be towed without checking its spin by attaching a magnetic grapple to its centre of rotation, and with the shipside attachment point also rotating so that the line would not twist-shorten and bring the alien craft crashing into *Descartes*' side. During the trip the larger ship's hyperdrive field could be expanded to enclose both vessels.

His chief concern was over the leak and his complete ignorance of how long a period the alien spacecraft had intended to stay in orbit. He had also, if he wanted to establish friendly relations with the people on Meatball, to make the correct decision quickly.

He knew that in the early days of human space-flight leakage was a quite normal occurrence, for there had been many occasions when it had been preferable to carry extra air supplies rather than pay the severe weight penalty of making the craft completely airtight. On the other hand the leak and spinning were more likely to be emergency conditions with the time available for their correction strictly limited. Since the alien astronaut or astronauts would not, for some odd reason, let him immobilise their ship to make a more thorough investigation of its condition and because he could not reproduce their environment anyway, his duty was plain. Probably his hesitancy was due to misplaced professional pride because he was passing responsibility for a particularly sticky one to others.

Quickly and with his usual economy of words the Captain issued the necessary orders and, less than half an hour after it had first been sighted the alien spacecraft was on its way to Sector General.

TWO

WITH quiet insistence the P.A. was repeating, "Will Senior Physician Conway please contact Major O'Mara ..."

Conway quickly sized up the traffic situation in the corridor, jumped across the path of a Tralthan intern who was lumbering down on him on six elephantine feet, rubbed fur briefly with a Kelgian caterpillar who was moving in the opposite direction and, while squeezing himself against the wall to avoid being run over by something in a highly refrigerated box on wheels, unracked the handset of the communicator.

As soon as he had established contact the P.A. began insisting quietly that somebody else contact somebody else.

"Are you doing anything important at the moment, Doctor?" asked the Chief Psychologist without preamble. "Engaged on vital research, perhaps, or in performing some life-or-death operation?" O'Mara paused, then added drily, "You realise, of course, that these questions are purely rhetorical . . ."

Conway sighed and said, "I was just going to lunch."

"Fine," said O'Mara. "In that case you will be delighted to know that the natives of Meatball have put a spacecraft into orbit—judging by its looks it may well be their first. It got into difficulties—Colonel Skempton can give you the details—and *Descartes* is bringing it here for us to deal with. It will arrive in just under three hours and I suggest you take an ambulance ship and heavy rescue gear out to it with a view to extricating its crew. I shall also suggest that Doctors Mannen and Prilicla be detached from their normal duties to assist you, since you three are going to be our specialists in Meatball matters."

"I understand," said Conway eagerly.

"Right," said the Major. "And I'm glad, Doctor, that you realise that there are things more important than food. A less enlightened and able psychologist than myself might wonder at this sudden hunger which develops whenever an important assignment is mentioned. I, of course, realise that this is not an outward symptom of a sense of insecurity but sheer, blasted greed!

"You will have arrangements to make, Doctor," he concluded pleasantly. "Off."

Conway left the communicator with mixed feelings. He was at once anxious about the coming meeting with the perhaps badly injured Meatball native and the problems of communication which were bound to arise, and glad that Mannen and Prilicla would be on hand to help. For when O'Mara made a "suggestion" it became nothing less than an entry in the pages of future history because, even though there were scores of officers in the Hospital who outranked him, the limits of the Major's authority were difficult to define.

As Chief Psychologist, O'Mara's prime concern was the efficient and smooth integration of its medical staff. But keeping so many different and potentially antagonistic life-forms working in harmony was not an easy job. Given even the highest qualities of tolerance and mutual respect in its personnel, potentially dangerous situations could still arise through ignorance or misunderstanding, or a being might suddenly develop a xenophobic neurosis which might affect its professional efficiency, mental stability or both. An Earth-human doctor, for instance, who had a subconscious fear of spiders would not be able to bring to bear on one of the insectile Cinrusskin patients the proper degree of clinical detachment necessary for its treatment. It was O'Mara's job to detect and eradicate such troubles, or in extreme cases to remove potentially troublesome in-dividualism and to this end he was given a large, and in many cases the final, say in which doctor was assigned where and to whom.

O'Mara's sarcastic disposition did not anger so much as irritate Conway, and then only slightly. For it was the generally held opinion that when O'Mara was polite and friendly and not at all sarcastic, when he began treating a person as a patient rather than a colleague in other words, that person was in serious trouble. When he was not un-duly concerned over an individual, or in some cases when he actually liked them, the psychologist felt able to relax with them and be his natural, bad-tempered self.

Skempton's office was fairly close so that Conway needed just fifteen minutes—which included the time taken to don a protective suit for the two hundred yards of the journey which lay through the levels of the Illensan chlorine-breathers—to reach it.

Sector General was supplied and to a large extent maintained by the Monitor Corps, which was the Federation's executive and law-enforcement arm. As the senior Corps officer in the hospital, Colonel Skempton handled all traffic to and from the establishment together with a horde of other administrative details. The Colonel was a very busy man, his time was valuable, and Conway intended being as brief as possible . . .

"Good morning," said Skempton while Conway was still opening his mouth. "Tip the stuff off that chair and sit down. O'Mara has been in touch. I've decided to return *Descartes* to Meatball as soon as it leaves the distressed spacecraft. To native observers it might appear that the vehicle was taken—one might almost say kidnapped—and *Descartes* should be on hand to note reactions, make contact if possible and give reassurances. I'd be obliged if you would extricate, treat and return this patient to Meatball as quickly as possible—you can imagine the boon this would be to our cultural contact people.

"This is a copy of the report on the incident radioed from *Descartes*," the Colonel went on without, apparently, even pausing for breath. "And you will need this analysis of water taken from the sea around the take-off—the actual samples will be available as soon as *Descartes* arrives. Should you need further background information on Meatball or on contact procedures call on Lieutenant Harrison, who is due for discharge now and who will be glad to assist. Try not to slam the door, Doctor."

The Colonel began excavating deeply in the layer of paperwork covering his desk and Conway closed his mouth again and left. In the outer office he asked permission to use the communicator and got to work.

An unoccupied ward in the Chalder section was the obvious place to house the new patient. The giant denizens of Chalderescol 11 were water-breathers, although the tepid, greenish water in which they lived was almost one hundred per cent pure compared with the soupy environment of Meatball's seas. The analysis would allow Dietetics and Environmental Control to synthesise the food content of the water—but not to reproduce the living organisms it contained. That would have to wait until the samples arrived and they had a chance to study and breed these organisms, just as the E.C. people could reproduce the gravity and water pressure, but would have to wait for the arrival of the spacecraft to add the finishing touches to the patient's quarters.

Next he arranged for an ambulance ship with heavy rescue equipment, crew and medical support to be made available prior to *Descartes'* arrival. The tender should be prepared to transfer a patient of unknown physiological classification who was probably injured and decompressed and close to terminal by this time, and he wanted a rescue team experienced in the rapid emergency transfer of ship-wreck survivors.

Conway was about to make a final call, to Thornnastor, the Diagnostician-in-Charge of Pathology, when he hesitated.

He was not quite sure whether he wanted to ask a series of specific questions—even a series of hypothetical questions—or to indulge in several minutes worrying out loud. It was vitally important that he treat and cure this patient. Quite apart from it being his and the hospital's job to do so, successful treatment would be the ideal way of opening communications with the natives of Meatball and ultimately laying hands on more of those wonderful, thought-controlled surgical instruments.

But what were the owners of those fabulous tools really like? Were they small and completely unspecialised with no fixed physical shape like the tools they used or, considering the mental abilities needed to develop the tools in the first place, were they little more than physically helpless brains dependent on their thought-controlled instruments to feed them, protect them and furnish all their physical needs? Conway badly wanted to know what to expect when the ship arrived. But Diagnosticians, as everyone knew, were unpredictable and even more impatient of muddy or confused thinking than was the Chief Psychologist.

The hospital was equipped to treat every known form of intelligent life, but no single person could hold in his brain even a fraction of the physiological data necessary for this purpose. Surgical dexterity was, of course, a matter of ability and training, but the complete physiological knowledge of any patient was furnished by means of an Educator Tape, which was simply the brain record of some great medical genius belonging to the same or a similar species to that of the patient being treated. If an Earth-human doctor had to treat a Kelgian patient he took one of that species' physiology tapes until treatment was complete, after which it was erased. The only exceptions to this rule were Senior Physicians with teaching duties and the Diagnosticians.

A Diagnostician was one of the Hospital's *elite*, a being whose mind was considered stable enough to retain six, seven and in some cases ten physiology tapes simultaneously. To their data-crammed minds were given the job of original research in xenological medicine and the treatment of new diseases in hitherto unknown life-forms. But the tapes did not impart only the physiological data—the complete memory and personality of the entity who had possessed that knowledge was transferred as well. In effect a Diagnostician subjected himself or itself voluntarily to the most drastic form of schizophrenia, and the entities apparently sharing the mind could be most unpleasant and aggressive individuals—geniuses were not as a rule charming people, and neither were Diagnosticians.

He would be better advised, Conway told himself, to let his questions wait until he had actually seen his patient, which would be in just over an hour from now. The intervening period he would spend studying *Descartes'* report.

And having lunch.

THREE

THE Monitor Survey cruiser popped into normal space, the alien spacecraft spinning like an unwieldy propeller astern, then just as quickly re-entered hyperspace for the return trip to Meatball. The rescue tender closed in, snagged the towline which had been left by *Descartes* and fixed the free end to a rotating attachment point of its own.

Spacesuited Doctors Mannen and Prilicla, Lieutenant Harrison and Conway watched from the tender's open airlock.

"It's still leaking," said Mannen. "That's a good sign—there is still pressure inside . . ."

"Unless it's a fuel leak," Harrison said.

"What do you feel?" asked Conway.

Prilicla's fragile, eggshell body and six pipe-stem legs were beginning to quiver violently so it was obvious that it was feeling something.

Conway felt sorry for the little being at times like these. Prilicla was a Cinrusskin of physiological classification GLNO—insectile, exoskeletal and possessing a highly developed empathic faculty, only on Cinruss with its feeble gravity could a race of insects have grown to such dimensions and evolved intelligence. Prilicla, because of its empathic faculty, was without doubt the most well-liked entity in the whole hospital, because the little being invariably did and said the right thing to everyone—being an emotion-sensitive, to do otherwise would mean that the feelings of anger or sorrow which a thoughtless word or action caused would bounce back and figuratively smack it in the face. So the little empath had no choice but to be invariably kind and considerate in order to make the emotional radiation of the beings around it as pleasant for itself as possible.

Except when its professional duties exposed it to pain and violent emotion during the treatment of a patient . . .

"The vessel contains one living entity," said Prilicla slowly. "Its emotional radiation is comprised chiefly of fear and feelings of pain and suffocation. I would say that these feelings have been with it for many days—the radiation is subdued and lacking in clarity due to developing unconsciousness. But the quality of that entity's mentation leaves no doubt that it is intelligent and not simply an experimental animal . . ."

"It's nice to know," said Mannen drily, "that we're not going to all this trouble for an instrument package or a Meatball space puppy . . ."

"We haven't much time," said Conway.

He was thinking that their patient must be pretty far gone by now. Its fear was understandable, of course, and its pain, suffocation and diminished consciousness were probably due to injury, intense hunger and foul breathing water. He tried to put himself in the Meatball astronaut's position.

Even though the pilot had been badly confused by the apparently uncontrollable spinning, the being had deliberately sought to maintain the spin when *Descartes* tried to take it aboard because it must have been smart enough to realise that a tumbling ship could not be drawn into the cruiser's hold. Possibly it could have checked its own spin with steering power if *Descartes* had not been so eager to rush to its aid—but that was simply a possibility, of course, and the spacecraft had been leaking badly as well. Now it was still leaking and spinning and, with its occupant barely conscious, Conway thought he could risk frightening it just a little more by checking the spin and moving the vehicle into the tender and the patient as quickly as possible into the water-filled compartment where they could work on it.

But as soon as the immaterial fingers of the tractor beams reached out an equally invisible force seemed to grip Prilicla's fragile body and shake it furiously.

"Doctor," said the empath, "the being is radiating extreme fear. It is forcing coherent thought from a mind which is close to panic. It is losing consciousness rapidly, perhaps dying . . . Look! It is using steering thrust!"

"*Cut!*" shouted Conway to the tractor beamers. The alien spacecraft, which had almost come to rest, began to spin slowly as vapour jetted from lateral vents in the nose and stern. After a few minutes the jets became irregular, weaker and finally ceased altogether, leaving the vehicle spinning at approximately half its original speed. Prilicla still looked as if its body was being shaken by a high wind.

"Doctor," said Conway suddenly, "considering the kind of tools these people use I wonder if some kind of psionic force is being used against you—you are shaking like a leaf."

When it replied Prilicla's voice was devoid of all emotion —the words, which were being transmitted to the gigantic translation computer in the bowels of the hospital then redirected to Conway's translator pack, had had all warmth and tonal variation filtered out of them.

"It is not thinking directly at anyone, friend Conway," said the empath. "Its emotional radiation is composed chiefly of fear and despair. Perceptions are diminishing and it seems to be struggling to avoid a final catastrophe . . ."

"Are you thinking what I'm thinking?" said Mannen suddenly.

"If you mean am I thinking of setting the thing spinning

28

at full speed again," Conway replied, "the answer is yes. But there's no logical reason for doing so, is there?'

A few seconds later the tractor beam men reversed polarity to increase the vessel's spin. Almost immediately Prilicla's trembling ceased and it said, "The being feels much better now—relatively, that is. Its vitality is still very low."

Prilicla began to tremble again and this time Conway knew that his own feelings of angry frustration were affecting the little being. He tried to make his thinking cooler and more constructive, even though he knew that the situation was essentially the same as it had been when *Descartes* had first tried to aid the Meatball astronaut, that they were making no progress at all.

But there were a few things he could do which would help the patient, however indirectly.

The vapour escaping from the vehicle should be analysed to see if it was fuel or simply water from the being's life-support system. Much valuable data could be gained from a direct look at the patient—even if it was only possible to see it through the wrong end of a periscope, since the vessel did not possess a direct vision port. They should also seek means of entering the vessel to examine and reassure the occupant before transferring it to the ambulance and the wards.

Closely followed by Lieutenant Harrison, Conway pulled himself along the towing cable towards the spinning ship. By the time they had gone a few yards both men were turning with the rotating cable so that when they reached the spacecraft it seemed steady while the rest of creation whirled around them in dizzying circles. Mannen stayed in the airlock, insisting that he was too old for such acrobatics, and Prilicla approached the vessel drifting free and using its spacesuit propulsors for manoeuvring.

Now that the patient was almost unconscious the Cin-

29

russkin had to be close to detect subtle changes in its emotional radiation. But the long, tubular hull was hurtling silently past the little being like the vanes of some tremendous windmill.

Conway did not voice his concern, however. With Prilicla one did not need to.

"I appreciate your feelings, friend Conway," said Prilicla, "but I do not think that I was born, despite my physiological classification, to be swatted."

At the hull they transferred from the towing cable and used wrist and boot magnets to cling to the spinning ship, noting that the magnetic grapple placed there by *Descartes* had seriously dented the hull plating and that the area was obscured by a fog of escaping vapour. Their own suit magnets left shallow grooves in the plating as well. The mental was not much thicker than paper, and Conway felt that if he made a too-sudden movement he would kick a hole in it.

"It isn't quite as bad as that, Doctor," said the Lieutenant. "In our own early days of spaceflight—before gravity control, hyperspatial travel and atomic motors made considerations of weight of little or no importance—vehicles had to be built as light as possible. So much so that the fuel contents were sometimes used to help stiffen the structure . . ."

"Nevertheless," said Conway, "I feel as if I am lying on very thin ice—I can even hear water or fuel gurgling underneath. Will you check the stern, please. I'll head forward."

They took samples of the escaping vapour from several points and they tapped and sounded and listened carefully with sensitive microphones to the noises coming from inside the ship. There was no response from the occupant, and Prilicla told them that it was unaware of their presence. The only signs of life from the interior were mechanical. There seemed to be an unusually large amount of machinery, to judge from the sounds they could hear, in addition to the gurgling of liquid. And as they moved towards the extremities of the vessel, centrifugal force added another complication.

The closer they moved towards the bow or stern, the greater was the force tending to fling them off the spinning ship.

Conway's head was pointing towards the ship's bow so that the centrifugal force was imposing a negative G on his body. It was not really uncomfortable as yet, however—he felt a little pop-eyed but there was no redding out of vision. His greatest discomfort came from the sight of the ambulance ship, Prilicla and the vast, tubular Christmas tree which was Sector General sweeping around the apparently steady ship's bows. When he closed his eyes the feeling of vertigo diminished, but then he could not see what he was doing.

The farther forward he went the more power his suit magnets needed to hold him against the smooth metal of the ship's hull, but he could not increase the power too much because the thin plating was beginning to ripple under the magnets and he was afraid of tearing open the hull. But a few feet ahead there was a stubby, projecting pipe which was possibly some kind of periscope and he began to slide himself carefully towards it. Suddenly he began to slip forward and grabbed instinctively for the pipe as he slithered past.

The projection bent alarmingly in his hand and he let go hurriedly, noticing the cloud of vapour which had formed around it, and he felt himself being flung away like a stone from a slingshot.

"Where the blazes are you, Doctor?" said Mannen. "Last time around you were there, now you aren't . . ."

"I don't know, Doctor," Conway replied angrily. He lit

31

one of his suit's distress flares and added, "Can you see me now?"

As he felt the tractor beams focus on him and begin to draw him back to the tender, Conway went on, "This is ridiculous! We're taking far too long over what should be a simple rescue job. Lieutenant Harrison and Doctor Prilicla, go back to the tender, please. We'll try another approach."

While they were discussing it Conway had the spacecraft photographed from every angle and had the tender's lab begin a detailed analysis of the samples Harrison and himself had gathered. They were still trying to find another approach when the prints and completed analyses reached them several hours later.

It had been established that all the leaks in the alien spacecraft were of water rather than fuel, that the water was for breathing purposes only since it did not contain the usual animal and vegetable matter found in the Meatball ocean samples and that, compared with these local samples, its CO_2 content was rather high—the water was, in brief, dangerously stale.

A close study of the photographs by Harrison, who was quite an authority on early spaceflight, suggested that the flared-out stern of the ship contained a heat shield to which was mounted a solid fuel retro pack. It was now plain that, rather than an unignited final stage, the long cylindrical vehicle contained little more than the life-support equipment which, judging by its size, must be pretty crude. Having made this statement the Lieutenant promptly had second, more charitable thoughts and added that while air-breathing astronauts could carry compressed air with them a water-breather could not very well compress its water.

The point of the nose cone contained small panels which would probably open to release the landing parachutes. About five feet astern of this was another panel which was about fifteen inches wide and six feet deep. This was an odd shape for an entry and exit hatch for the pilot, but Harrison was convinced that it could be nothing else. He added that the lack of sophistication shown in the vehicle's construction made it unlikely that the exit panel was the outer seal of an airlock, that it was almost certainly a simple hatch opening into the command module.

If Doctor Conway was to open this hatch, he warned, centrifugal force would empty the ship of its water—or to be quite accurate, of half its water—within a few seconds. The same force would see to it that the water in the stern section remained there, but it was almost certain that the astronaut was in the nose cone.

Conway yawned furiously and rubbed his eyes. He said, "I have to see the patient to get some idea of its injuries and to prepare accommodation, Lieutenant. Suppose I cut a way in amidships at the centre of rotation. An appreciable quantity of its water has already leaked away and centrifugal force has caused the remainder to be pushed towards the nose and stern, so that the middle of the ship would be empty and the additional loss of water caused by my entry would be slight."

"I agree, Doctor," said Harrison. "But the structure of the ship might be such that you would open a seam into the water-filled sections—it's so fragile there is even the danger that centrifugal force might pull it apart."

Conway shook his head. "If we put a wide, thin-metal band around the waist section, and if the band included a hinged, airtight hatch big enough for a man, we can seal the edges of the band to the ship with fast-setting cement—no welding, of course, as the heat might damage the skin—and rig a temporary airlock over the hatch. That would allow me to get in without——"

"That would be a very tricky job," said Mannen, "on a spinning ship."

Harrison said, "Yes. But we can set up a light, tubular framework anchored to the hull by magnets. The band and airlock could be set up working from that. It will take a little time, though."

Prilicla did not comment. Cinrusskins were notoriously lacking in physical stamina and the little empath had attached itself to the ceiling with six, sucker-tipped legs and had gone to sleep.

Mannen, the Lieutenant and Conway were ordering material and specialised assistance from the Hospital and beginning to organise a work party when the tender's radioman said, "I have Major O'Mara for you on screen Two."

"Doctor Conway," said the Chief Psychologist, when he was able to see and be seen. "Rumours have reached me that you are trying—and may have already succeeded, in fact—to set up a new record for the length of time taken to transfer a patient from ship to ward. I have no need to remind you of the urgency and importance of this matter, but I will anyway. It is urgent, Doctor, and important. Off."

"You sarcastic . . ." began Conway angrily to the already fading image, then quickly controlled his feelings because they were beginning to make Prilicla twitch in its sleep.

"Maybe," said the Lieutenant, looking speculatively at Mannen, "my leg isn't properly healed since I broke it during that landing on Meatball. A friendly, cooperative Doctor might decide to send me back to Level Two-eighty-three, Ward Four."

"The same friendly, helpful Doctor," said Mannen drily, "might decide a certain Earth-human nurse in 283-Four had something to do with your relapse, and he might send you to . . . say, 241-Seven. There is nothing like being fussed over by a nurse with four eyes and far too many legs to cure a man of baying at the moon."

Conway laughed. "Ignore him, Harrison. At times his

mind is even nastier than O'Mara's. Right now there isn't anything more we can do and it has been a long, hard day. Let's go to bed before we go to sleep."

Four

ANOTHER day went by without any significant progress being made. Because of the need for urgency the team setting up the framework tried to hurry the job, with the result that they lost tools, sections of framework and on several occasions men overboard. The men could be retrieved easily enough by tractor beams, but the tools and framework sections were not equipped with signal flares and were usually lost. Cursing the necessity for having to perform a tricky job of construction on a space-going merry-go-round, the men went back to work.

Progress became much slower but a little more certain, the number of dents and furrows put in the spacecraft's hull by tools and space-boots had become uncountable, and the fog of water vapour escaping from the vessel continued to increase.

In a desperate attempt to speed things up, and much against Prilicla's wishes, Conway tried slowing the craft's rate of spin again. There were no signs of panic from the occupant this time, the empath reported, because it was too deeply unconscious to care. It added that it could not describe the patient's emotional radiation to anyone but another empath, but that it was its considered professional opinion that if full spin was not restored the patient would die very shortly.

Next day the framework was completed and work started on fitting the metal band which would take the temporary airlock. While the lock structure was going up Conway and Harrison attached safety lines to the framework and examined the hull. The Lieutenant discovered

35

quite a lot about the steering jets and the circuits to the retro pack, while Conway could only stare baffled at the long, narrow exit hatch or stare through the tiny glass port—it was only a few inches in diameter—which showed little more than a shutter which opened and closed rapidly. And it was not until the following day that the Lieutenant and himself were able to enter the alien spacecraft.

Its occupant was still alive, Prilicla said, but only just.

As expected the waist section of the spacecraft was almost empty of water. Centrifugal force had caused it to collect towards the extremities of the ship, but their spotlights reflected off a dazzling fog of water vapour and droplets which, a quick investigation showed, were being stirred up by the operation of a system of sprocket wheels and chain drives that ran the length of the ship.

Moving carefully so as not to snag a hand between a gear wheel and its chain or inadvertently stick a boot through the fragile hull into space, the Lieutenant moved aft while Conway went forward. They did this so as to ensure that the vessel's centre of gravity stayed as closely as possible to its centre of rotation, for any imbalance introduced now would shake loose the framework and probably tear holes in the sides of the ship.

"I realise that the circulation and purification of water requires heavier hardware than an air recycling system," said Conway, speaking to Harrison and the tender, "but surely there should be a higher proportion of electrical to mechanical systems? I can't move more than a few yards forward and all I can see are gear wheels and chain drives. The circulation system sets up a strong current, as well, and I'm in danger of being drawn into the works."

The fine, ever-present mist of bubbles made it difficult to see clearly, but for a moment he caught a glimpse of something which was not part of the machinery—something that was brown and convoluted and with a suggestion of fronds

36

or short tentacles sprouting from it, something organic. The being was hemmed in on all sides by revolving machinery, and it also seemed to be rotating, but there was so little of its body visible that he could not be sure.

"I see it," said Conway. "Not enough for accurate classification, though. It doesn't seem to be wearing a pressure suit so this must be its equivalent of shirt-sleeves conditions. But we can't get at the brute without tearing its ship apart and killing it in the process." He swore, then went on furiously, "This is ridiculous, insane! I'm supposed to come out here, immobilise the patient, transfer it to a ward and give treatment. But this blasted thing *can't* be immobilised without . . ."

"Suppose there is something wrong with its life-support system," the Lieutenant broke in. "Something which requires gravity, or artificial gravity in the form of centrifugal force, to restore proper function. If we could somehow repair this malfunctioning equipment . . ."

"But why?" said Conway suddenly, as a vague idea that had been lurking at the back of his mind began to creep out into the light. "I mean, why should we assume that it is malfunctioning . . ." He paused, then said, "We'll open the valves of a couple of oxygen tanks in here to freshen up the beastie's air—I mean water. It's only a first aid measure, I'm afraid, until we're in a position to do something more positive. Then back to the tender, I'm beginning to get some odd ideas about this astronaut and I'd like to test them."

They returned to the control-room without taking off their suits, and were met by Prilicla who told them that the patient's condition seemed a little better although it was still unconscious. The empath added that the reason for this might be that the being was injured and in an advanced state of malnutrition as well as having been close to death through asphyxiation. Conway began telling them about his idea and sketching the alien ship as he talked.

"If this is the centre of spin," he said when the drawing was complete, "and the distance from that point to the pilot's position is this, and the rate of rotation is this, can you tell me how closely does the apparent gravity in the pilot's position approach that of Meatball itself?"

"Just a minute," said Harrison as he took Conway's pen and began to scribble. A few minutes later—he had taken extra time to double check his calculations—he said, "Very close, Doctor. Identical, in fact."

"Which means," said Conway thoughtfully, "that we have here a beastie which can't, for some very good physiological reason no doubt, live without gravity, for whom weightless conditions are fatal . . ."

"Excuse me, Doctor," the quiet voice of the radioman cut in. "I have Major O'Mara for you on screen Two . . ."

Conway felt the idea which was beginning to take shape at the back of his mind being blown into tatters. *Spin*, he thought furiously, trying to draw it back; *centrifugal force, wheels within wheels!* But the square, craggy features of the Chief Psychologist were filling the screen and it was impossible to think of anything else.

O'Mara spoke pleasantly, which was a very bad sign. He said, "Your recent activity has been impressive, Doctor—especially when it took the form of man-made meteorite activity in the shape of dropped tools and structural material. But I'm concerned about your patient. We all are—even, and especially, the Captain of *Descartes* who has recently returned to Meatball.

"The Captain has run into trouble," the psychologist continued, "in the shape of three missiles with nuclear warheads which were directed at his ship. One of them went off course and dirtied up a large area of Meatball ocean, and the other two came so close that he had to use full emergency thrust to avoid them. He says that establishing communications and friendly contact with the inhabitants in these circumstances is impossible, that they obviously think he has kidnapped their astronaut for some ghastly purpose of his own, and that the return of the being in a happy and healthy condition is the only means there is of retrieving the situation . . . Doctor Conway, your mouth is open. Either say something or close it!"

"Sorry, sir," said Conway absently. "I was thinking. There is something I would like to try, and perhaps you could help me with it—by getting Colonel Skempton's support, I mean. We're wasting time out here, I realise that now, and I want to bring the spacecraft inside the hospital. Still spinning, of course—at first, anyway. Cargo Lock Thirty is big enough to take it and is close enough to the water-filled corridor leading to the ward we are preparing for this patient. But I'm afraid the Colonel will be a bit sticky about allowing the spacecraft into the hospital."

The Colonel was very sticky indeed, despite Conway's arguments and the support given by O'Mara. Skempton, for the third time, gave a firm and unequivocal negative.

He said, "I realise the urgency of this matter. I fully appreciate its importance to our future hopes of trading with Meatball and I sympathise with your technical problems. But you are not, repeat not, going to bring a chemically powered spacecraft with a live retro pack inside this hospital! If it accidentally ignited we might have a hole blown in the hull which would cause a lethal pressure drop on a dozen levels, or the vehicle might go bulleting into the central computer or gravity control sections!"

"Excuse me," said Conway angrily, and turned to the Lieutenant. He asked, "Can you ignite that retro pack, working from the ambulance ship, or disconnect it?"

"I probably couldn't disconnect it without inadvertently setting it off and burning myself to a crisp," Harrison replied slowly, "but I know enough to be able to set up a relay which . . . Yes, we could ignite it from this control-room."

"Go to it, Lieutenant," said Conway, and returned to the image of Skempton. "I take it, sir, that you have no objection to taking the vessel aboard after its retro pack has been fired? Or to furnishing the special equipment I will need in the cargo lock and ward?"

"The maintenance officer on that level has orders to cooperate," said Skempton. "Good luck, Doctor. Off."

While Harrison set up his relay, Prilicla kept an emotional eye on the patient while Mannen and himself worked out the being's approximate size and weight based on the brief look Conway had had of the astronaut and on the dimensions of its ship. This information would be needed quickly if the special transporter and the rotating operating theatre were to be ready in time.

"I'm still here, Doctor," said O'Mara sharply, "and I have a question. Your idea that the being needs gravity, either normal or artificial, to live I can understand, but strapping it on to an elaborate merry-go-round . . ."

"Not a merry-go-round, sir," said Conway. "It will be mounted vertically, like a ferris wheel."

O'Mara breathed heavily through his nose. "I suppose you are quite sure that you know what you're doing, Doctor?"

"Well . . ." began Conway.

"Ask a stupid question," said the psychologist, and broke the connection.

FIVE

IT took longer than the Lieutenant had estimated to set up his relay—*everything* took longer than estimated on this assignment!—and Prilicla reported that the patient's condition was rapidly worsening. But at last the spacecraft's retros flared out for the number of seconds necessary to have brought it out of its original orbit and the ambulance ship kept pace with it, spinning it with opposing tractors as soon as thrust disappeared so that the occupant would still have the gravity it needed. There were complications even so. Immediately the retros cut out, panels opened in the nose cone and the landing parachute tumbled out and within seconds the spinning ship had wound the parachute untidily around itself.

The short period of thrust had added to the hull damage as well.

"It's leaking like a sieve!" Conway burst out. "Shoot another magnetic grapple to it. Keep it spinning and get us to Lock Thirty quick! How is the patient?"

"Conscious now," said Prilicla, trembling. "Just barely conscious and radiating extreme fear . . ."

Still spinning, the vehicle was manoeuvred into the enormous mouth of Lock Thirty. Inside the lock chamber the artificial gravity grids under the deck were set at neutral so that the weightless conditions of space were duplicated there. Conway's feeling of vertigo which had been with him since he had first seen the ship was intensified by the sight of the alien vessel whirling ponderously in the enclosed space, flinging out streamers of coldly steaming water as it spun.

Then suddenly the lock's outer seal clanged shut, the tractors smoothly checked the ship's spin as, simultaneously, the artificial gravity of the deck was brought up to Meatball normal. Within a few seconds the spacecraft was resting horizontally on the deck.

"How is it?" began Conway anxiously.

Prilicla said, "Fear . . . no, extreme anxiety. The radiation is quite strong now—otherwise the being seems all right, or at least improved . . ." The empath gave the impression of not believing its own feelings.

41

The spacecraft was lifted gently and a long, low trolley mounted on balloon wheels rolled under it. Water began pouring into the lock chamber from the seal which had opened into the adjacent water-filled section. Prilicla ran up the wall and across the ceiling until it was in position a few yards above the nose of the vessel, and Mannen, Harrison and Conway waded, then swam, in the same direction. When they reached it they clustered around the forward section, ignoring the team which was throwing straps around the hull and fastening it to the trolley prior to moving it into the nearby corridor of the water-breathers, while they cut into the thin hull plating and carefully peeled it away.

Conway insisted on extreme care during this operation so as to avoid damaging the life-support machinery.

Gradually the nose section became little more than a skeleton and the astronaut lay revealed, like a leathery, brown caterpillar with its tail in its mouth that was caught on one of the innermost gear wheels of a giant clock. By this time the vessel was completely submerged, oxygen was being released into the water all around it, and Prilicla was reporting the patient's feelings as being extremely anxious and confused.

"*It*'s confused . . ." said a familiar, irascible voice and Conway discovered O'Mara swimming beside him. Colonel Skempton was dog-paddling along on his other side, but silently. The psychologist went on, "This is an important one, Doctor, in case you've forgotten—hence our close personal interest. But now why don't you pull that glorified alarm clock apart and get the patient out of there? You've proved your theory that it needed gravity to live, and we're supplying that now . . ."

"No, sir," said Conway, "not just yet . . ."

"Obviously the rotation of the being inside the capsule," Colonel Skempton broke in, "compensates for the ship's spin, thus allowing the pilot a stationary view of the outside world."

"I don't know," said Conway doggedly. "The ship's rotation does not quite match that of the astronaut inside it. In my opinion we should wait until we can transfer it quickly to the ferris wheel, which will almost exactly duplicate module conditions. I have an idea—it may be a pretty wild one—that we aren't out of the woods yet."

"But transferring the whole ship into the ward when the patient alone could be moved there in a fraction of the time . . ."

"No," said Conway.

"He's the Doctor," said O'Mara, before the argument could develop further, and smoothly directed the Colonel's attention to the system of paddle-wheels which kept the water-breathing astronaut's "air" circulating.

The enormous trolley, its weight supported in the water to a large extent by air-filled balloon tyres, was manhandled along the corridor and into the tremendous tank which was one of the combined theatre/wards of the hospital's water-breathing patients. Suddenly there was another complication.

"Doctor! It's coming out!"

One of the men swarming around the nose section must have accidentally pushed the astronaut's ejection button, because the narrow hatch had swung open and the system of gears, sprocket wheels and chain drives was sliding into new positions. Something which looked like three five-foot diameter tyres was rolling towards the opening.

The innermost tyre of the three was the astronaut while the two on each side of it had a metallic look and a series of tubes running from them into the central, organic tyre—probably food storage tanks, Conway thought. His theory was borne out when the outer sections stopped just inside the hatch and the alien, still trailing one of the feeding

43

tubes, rolled out of its ship. Still turning it began to fall slowly towards the floor eight feet below.

Harrison, who was nearest, tried to break its fall but could only get one hand to it. The being tipped over and hit the floor flat on its side. It bounced slowly just once and came to rest, motionless.

"It is unconscious again, dying! Quickly, friend Conway!"

The normally polite and self-effacing empath had turned the volume of its suit radio to maximum so as to attract attention quickly. Conway acknowledged with a wave—he was already swimming towards the fallen astronaut as fast as he could—and yelled at Harrison, "Get it upright, man! Turn it!"

"What . . ." began Harrison, but he nevertheless got both hands under the alien and began to lift.

Mannen, O'Mara and Conway arrived together. With four of them working on it they quickly lifted the being into an upright position, but when Conway tried to get them to roll it, it wobbled like a huge, soggy hoop and tended to fold in on itself. Prilicla, at great danger to life and its extremely fragile limbs, landed beside them and deafened everyone with details of the astronaut's emotional radiation—which was now virtually non-existent.

Conway yelled directions to the other three to lift the alien to waist height while keeping it upright and turning. Within a few seconds he had O'Mara pulling down on his side, Mannen lifting on his and the Lieutenant and himself at each flank turning and steadying the great, flaccid, ring-shaped body.

"Cut your volume, Prilicla!" O'Mara shouted. Then in a quieter, furious voice he snarled, "I suppose one of us knows what we're doing?"

"I think so," said Conway. "Can you speed it up—it was rotating much faster than this inside its ship. Prilicla?"

44

"It . . . it is barely alive, friend Conway."

They did everything possible to speed the alien's rotation while at the same time moving it towards the accommodation prepared for it. This contained the elaborate ferris wheel which Conway had ordered and a watery atmosphere which duplicated the soup of Meatball's oceans. It was not an exact duplicate because the material suspended in the soup was a non-living synthetic rather than the living organisms found in the original, but it had the same food value and, because it was non-toxic so far as the other water-breathers who were likely to use the ward were concerned, the astronaut's quarters were contained by a transparent plastic film rather than metal plating and a lock chamber. This also helped speed the process of getting the patient into its ward and on to the wheel.

Finally it was in position, strapped down and turning in the direction and at the same velocity as its "couch" on the spacecraft. Mannen, Prilicla and Conway attached themselves as close to the centre of the wheel and their rotating patient as possible and, as their examination proceeded, theatre staff, special instruments, diagnostic equipment and the very special, thought-controlled "tool" from Meatball added themselves or were attached to the framework of the wheel and whirled up and over and around through the nearly opaque soup.

The patient was still deeply unconscious at the end of the first hour.

For the benefit of O'Mara and Skempton, who had relinquished their places on the wheel to members of the theatre staff, Conway said, "Even at close range it is difficult to see through this stuff, but as the process of breathing is involuntary and includes ingestion, and as the patient has been short of food and air for a long time, I'd prefer not to work in clear, food-free water at this time."

"My favourite medicine," said Mannen, "is food."

"I keep wonderng how such a life-form got started," Conway went on. "I suppose it all began in some wide, shallow, tidal pool—so constituted that the tidal effects caused the water to wash constantly around it instead of going in and out. The patient might then have evolved from some early beastie which was continually rolled around in the shallows by the circular tides, picking up food as it went. Eventually this prehistoric beastie evolved specialised internal musculature and organs which allowed it to do the rolling instead of trusting to the tides and currents, also manipulatory appendages in the form of this fringe of short tentacles sprouting from the inner circumference of its body between the series of gill mouths and eyes—its visual equipment must operate like some form of coeleostat since the contents of its field of vision are constantly rotating.

"Reproduction is probably by direct fission," he went on, "and they keep rolling for every moment of their lives, because to stop is to die."

"But *why*?" O'Mara broke in. "Why must it roll when water and food can be sucked in without its having to move?"

"Do you know what is wrong wth the patient, Doctor?" Skempton asked sharply, then added worriedly, "Can you treat it?"

Mannen made a noise which could have been a snort of derision, a bark of laughter or perhaps merely a strangled cough.

Conway said, "Yes and no, sir. Or, in a sense, the answer should be yes to both questions." He glanced at O'Mara to include the psychologist and went on, "It has to roll to stay alive—there is an ingenious method of shifting its centre of gravity while keeping itself upright by partially inflating the section of its body which is on top at any given moment. The continual rolling causes its blood to circulate —it uses a form of gravity feed system instead of a

46

muscular pump. You see, this beastie has no heart, none at all. When it stops rolling its circulation stops and it dies within a few minutes.

"The trouble is," he ended grimly, "we may have almost stopped its circulation once too often."

"I disagree, friend Conway," said Prilicla, who never disagreed with anyone as a rule. The empath's body and pipestem legs were quivering, but slowly in the manner of a Cinrusskin who was being exposed to emotion of a type which was completely pleasant. It went on, "The patient is regaining consciousness quickly. It is fully conscious now. There is a suggestion of dull, unlocalised pain which is almost certainly caused by hunger, but this is already beginning to fade. It is feeling slightly anxious, very excited and intensely curious."

"Curious?" said Conway.

"Curiosity is the predominating emotion, Doctor."

"Our early astronauts," said O'Mara, "were very special people, too . . ."

It was more than an hour later by the time they were finished, medically speaking, with the Meatball astronaut and were climbing out of their suits. A Corps linguist was sharing the ferris wheel with the alien with the intention of adding, with the minimum of delay, a new e-t language to the memory banks of the hospital's translation computer, and Colonel Skempton had left to compose a rather tricky message to the Captain of *Descartes*.

"The news isn't all good," Conway said, grinning with relief despite himself. "For one thing, our 'patient' wasn't suffering from anything other than malnutrition, partial asphyxiation and general mishandling as a result of being rescued—or rather kidnapped—by *Descartes*. As well, it shows no special aptitude in the use of the thought-controlled tool we wish to trade for, although it seems to recognise the thing. This may mean that there is another

47

intelligent race on Meatball. But when our friend can talk properly to us I don't think there will be any difficulty getting it to introduce us to the real owners—it doesn't hold any grudges for the number of times we nearly killed it, Prilicla says, and . . . and I don't know how we managed to come out of this so well after all the stupid mistakes we made."

"And if you are trying to extract a compliment from me for another brilliant piece of deductive reasoning, or your lucky guess," said O'Mara sourly, "you are wasting your time and mine . . ."

Mannen said, "Let's all have lunch."

Turning to go, O'Mara said, "You know I don't eat in public—it gives the impression that I am an ordinary human being like everyone else. Besides, I'll be too busy working out a set of tests for yet another so-called intelligent species . . ."

VISIONS OF MONAD

by

M. JOHN HARRISON

A new British author, with a brilliant piece of modern writing, takes a look at the "inner space" of the mind as his central character makes the transition from reality to unreality. Or could it be the other way round?

VISIONS OF MONAD

ONE : IDENTITY

Bailey: supine on the studio floor—head pillowed on hands, phallic cigarette—watching the girl Monad apply paint, to ten square feet of canvas with a palette knife. Monad: nineteen and self-possessed, painting with her whole organism, in swift, precise movements; Monad in pale blue, nubile.

IT was late afternoon. The light in the studio was turning brown : puddles of late-September sun dappled his scruffy clothing. Bailey had done nothing all day but lie on the floor, smoking steadily, near to unconsciousness. Nor had he done anything more than eat or sprawl on the studio floor or make love in a lax, inert fashion for a week. Lately he had taken to sleeping for thirteen hours out of the twenty-four.

By contrast, the girl had filled half her canvas. Her technique was good—positive and self-possessed as her body—but her objective was unclear. In all probability, another week would elapse before anything coalesced from the slash of chaos on the canvas. Bailey was not interested in the process of creation. He would view the result with the eye of a professional, and she would bow to his judgment, accepting the validity of his critique without question. Because of this submission in the face of authoritative sources, she had little chance of becoming a true artist.

Bailey knew this, but did not tell her. Until such time as the picture was complete, he would remain silent. S.D. had left him very little concern with such matters. Since leaving the Institute he had not touched a brush. He had abandoned his own studio in Holloway.

He saw himself as caught in a twilight period; an Orpheus of the concrete city, suspended between the Hades of Sensory Deprivation and full, sterile awareness of the outer world. His psyche hung in a limbo fashioned partly from the total awareness of itself to be found in the Tank—with its lack of tactile sensation, its constant subliminal noise level, and its amorphous lighting—and partly from the complete perception of things to be found in the loud life of the city. Consequently, he lacked drive.

He had left the Holloway flat for two reasons. Hollis, who headed the S.D. research team at the Institute in W.1, had been pestering him with daily tests—orientation, motor response and the like—and he had become angry with this nagging interruption of his thought processes. The second reason was less concrete and by far the more powerful of the two. He had felt an indefinable need for a liaison, and a need to forge a link between his wandering mind—floating, drifting in its amniotic fluid of ab-reality—and the city. Monad, who loved him, had become that link, an anchor-chain mooring him to the reality of her society, her beatnik painters and poets and parties. He had moved in with her and refused even to return to Holloway to collect his mail.

His lassitude had ceased to worry him over much. At first he had tried to defeat it, and had returned to his earlier love of poetry when painting ceased to interest him. He had immersed himself in the works of Eliot and Thomas, and attempted to exorcise the blankness in his head by writing it down. He had finally given up. His last poem, an attempt to carry the work of the pre-nineteen-fourteen Imagists to its fullest extent, had read, simply :

gethsemane

He had begun to realise his problem, then. He had gone into the S.D. experiment to escape the broil of conflicting actions and concepts in which the city had threatened to suffocate him : he had come out of it with Nirvana—and a vision.

So he lay on the studio floor as the light turned brown, watching Monad's body. When it became too dark to paint, they ate and then made love. Monad was happy.

Morning. Monad in pale blue, shopping in a supermarket. Monad among the chattering, dull women, a denim-hipster dryad. Bailey: lying on the double bed, watching his hands tremble and not seeing them.

When the girl suggested a shopping expedition, Bailey roused himself from his torpor and agreed. He got as far as donning his battered cord jacket and walking with her to the front door. But the door opened on the street and the perspective of the street brought on his vision. The shift, the change of key was as immediate as a tropical dawn : the street—a perfectly ordinary brown stone hangover from Victoriana—faded into *the* street, the long, sweeping vee of his hallucination. He shook his head wordlessly at her. She nodded sympathetically and flirted off alone, swinging the shopping bag to some young girl's rhythm in her head.

Bailey shut the door after her and leant on it for a minute before he made his way carefully up the stairs. He *had* to be careful; not only did the stairs get mixed up with the vision; becoming a sort of out-of-phase corollary of it; forcing him to consider whether he was placing his feet on them or some miasma in his head : but also, the return of the hallucination always stimulated certain motor defects that had originated from his stay in the Tank. After the experiment, he had been unable to walk a straight line; he now had difficulty in guiding his foot to the next step of the stair. Some curiously detached part of him laughed dryly : Hollis would probably blow a fuse if he could measure Bailey's hand-tremor rate at this moment. There was no doubt that sustained sensory deprivation had a far more lasting physical effect than Hollis had suspected.

He sank on to the bed and relaxed his grip, allowing the hallucination to swamp him. Exterior noise—the rumble of heavy waggons on the main North Circular drag, shouts of children in a school yard—cut out completely. He watched the bedroom fade from around him. First, the titles of the books on the shelf : Robert Gittings on Keats became a dark blur, Tolkien's *Lord of the Rings* a red one; the shelf slowly sidled out of existence. The nude portrait of Monad above it followed. The last thing to go, sucked into greyness, was Monad's joke. Written in four-inch block-capitals on a sheet of white card, it was placed on the north wall, facing him. The legend exclaimed irreverently :

IT'S ALL STOPPED HAPPENING

Monad's appreciation of sexual innuendo was overt.

Then there was nothing but the hallucination, etched in grey-green on grey.

Bailey was standing in the middle of a road. His feet were placed on either side of the unbroken white line which extended in front of him without a curve. The horizon, too, was a perfectly straight line, clearly visible and unfogged by distance; an horizon a child might have drawn, dividing its picture into two equal, symmetrical rectangles. It existed merely as a dividing line : a separation of empty, light-grey sky and sick-green earth.

This sharp definition was repeated where the sides of the road met its surroundings. There was no sign of a kerb; nor was there gutter or peripheral vegetation : solely a precise, geometrical line.

Visually, that was all—a flat, three-tone landscape, unrelieved by vegetation or building; the white line running unbroken up the centre of the road to its vanishing point.

However, the Perspective—Bailey's mental shorthand describing the whole sensation—was not completely visual. There were auditory and tactile manifestations as well. As soon as the noises of the city faded, and usually before the visual component of the dream was anything like completed, Bailey would become aware of the wind at his back. It was cold and hard, and it sang : a single, clear, unadulterated note.

The dream became reality. Slowly and stiffly, Bailey, impelled by something nameless within himself, unable to contradict its orders, began to walk towards the vanishing point of the road. The wind pushed him steadily along, a cold hand in the small of his back. The objective side of his mind stopped commenting on the scene from its vantage-point of consciousness and turned subjective. Utterly caught up, he walked without thinking anything . . .

He had been walking for an hour when Monad reasserted the other reality, the existence-pattern of the "normal" world. She shook him gently and he stopped stumping fixedly to the unmentionable vanishing point. The wind died. There was a moment of disorientation in which he struggled to be part of one continuum or the other, flailing with his limbs to establish his whereabouts in space and time. Then, as he succeeded in focusing the microscope of his mind, the bedroom swam into sudden clarity. He looked with interest at its walls, as if they were new to him, noticing the details he had not seen before. There were faults in the study of Monad. He tried to remember who had painted it.

The girl took his trembling hands to her breast, warming

55

them. They were not trembling through cold, but the maternal gesture was gratifying. Suddenly, he remembered who he was and what he had been doing, and for some reason the knowledge made him cry like a baby.

Monad the hostess, in a studio full of people: talking animatedly of Bailey, as if she possessed him. Bailey: lounging with the inevitable cigarette, surrounded by beards and corduroy trousers—half-listening to young men discussing his poetry. Monad: out of denims for once: Monad the nymphette in a pale blue shift of silk, college-girl-madonna.

Earlier that day—the second after Bailey's latest walk along the perspective—the girl had scribbled: HAPPY BIRTH-DAY, HIROSHIMA on the studio wall and invited a gaggle of intellectuals to a party. There were about thirty people crammed into the room, mostly earnest young men from art colleges. A good proportion of them had gravitated towards Bailey to compliment him loudly on his recently published *Recollections of a Piebald Unicorn*. He found their vital, enthusiastic attention pleasing, but was embarrassed to discover that he could not recall half the poems in the slim volume. They were all relics of his pre-S.D. days; hard to reach. His experiences in the Tank had blocked off a great deal of his memory. Another thing, he reflected, that Hollis had neglected to investigate.

Paradoxically, the large amount of whisky he had drunk, had, far from numbing his brain, brought him one of the moments of insight he experienced with mounting infrequency. He began to ponder. *Exactly* why had he consented to take part in the sensory deprivation experiment? Precisely what had driven him to seek two weeks isolation from the world and forced him into the negative stimulus of the Tank? The young men were eclipsed much as the bedroom had been two days earlier. He concentrated. The answer came readily, but it was not simple.

There had been . . . too much.

He had been . . . sick; ill with the complexity of life; a malady with the city as its symbol. Pleased by this vague success, he began to probe for a tangible, a more solid memory upon which to found the architecture of his rejection of the things that had surrounded him. He delved, and came up with the diary. At first, he could picture only its cover and spiral binding. He took another drink and deliberately let the image of the book blot out his environment. Then, having satisfied himself that the memory would not dissolve, he reached out delicately and opened it.

January 7: . . . finding it more and more difficult to sleep; my brain rushing round in neurotic circles; thoughts like a speeded-up tape recording, gibberish until I (I? No. Until Gardner's depressants . . .) slow them down. The city has revealed itself as the nigger in this stockpile; although whether it is actually the root of the malaise, or just a convenient scapegoat upon which I project my inner turbulence, I cannot tell . . .

January 13: At its simplest level, the city is a maze in four dimensions, a purely physical ant-heap; over-large, over-complex and over-populated. I am continually frightened that the size and complexity of the hive will one day cause it to implode, to fall in on itself in a million slivers of coloured glass and lumps of rotting concrete. Yet, this fear aside, I catch myself wishing it would do just that: anything to escape this incredible multiplicity of directions and vectors. I hardly dare leave the studio; outside, it becomes impossible to choose from a thousand ways to go; I lose my identity immediately and travel blindly, in a frantic nightmare of Underground maps and back streets. This morning

I set out for Reynolds the Publishers in East 4, with the "Unicorn" manuscript. I came to in Kingsbury, shivering feverishly and wondering why I had gone there.

January 15: The cause–effect relationship is distorted surrealistically among all these lives and thought-patterns. Nudge a man in Greek Street, Soho, and he falls off a pavement in Plumstead; drop a stone in the Serpentine and a ship goes down in an Adriatic storm; bombard your target nucleus with neutrons and happy anniversary Nagasaki. Every action presents myriad side-effects, which are unpredictable. I cannot make a decision for fear of its unnoticed, incalculable results.

February 1: This *must* stop. Gardner the head-doctor tells me to leave the city before I break down (Before? He has yet to see me at night, wincing and twitching at every sound . . .) Today he brought with him a man called Hollis who thinks he can help me. I must be taking up too much of Gardner's time for him to fob me off with some pinchpenny researcher who can't afford to buy a subject for his experiment.

Hollis outlined his ideas as neatly and precisely as he is groomed and tailored. Unlike Gardner, who acknowledges art, he is the brusque, clipped epitome of science; the all-British owl-eye of the indigestion advertisements. I asked him why he hadn't gone to the spiritual mecca of all researchers, across the big water, and he started a long spiel on Britain's world-position before he realised that I was gently sending him up. The temperature of the room dropped considerably.

However, to give credit where it is due, his experiment is attractive: it offers a fixed course, or at least, a chance to search for one. There is a possibility that during the experimental period I will be able to pin down a concept that does not have as many heads as a hydra. Hollis warned me

58

that no one is quite sure of what effects sustained discon-
nection from reality will have on a person. I am afraid I
earned another black mark by laughing at him . . .

Bailey allowed the diary to fade out. The party took its
place, noisily. Somebody refilled his glass. He considered his
position, relating it to the events leading up to Hollis's
appearance.

Obviously, he had found his "concept" in the Tank. Its
representation, its ideograph, was the Perspective. Unfortunately, it seemed to have become as much of a fixation as
had the complexity of the city before it. He was strangely
unmoved by the knowledge that he had exchanged one
neurosis for another, a frenetic maelstrom for a degenerate
stasis. He ignored it in favour of a question that had flashed,
vivid and unbidden into his brain—

What would happen if he reached the vanishing point?
The prospect was fascinating.

TWO : NATIVITY

*Extracts from the private journal of Dr. James Hollis, Head
of Dept. 4, the Guirand Institute, London, England:*

February the fifth: B. arrived at the institute this morning, disguising his almost pitiful gratitude for this opportunity under a thin cloak of artistic smugness. He was
examined during the day and found to be in only mediocre
physical shape. He is, as Gardner noted, extremely disturbed and on the verge of nervous collapse. I begin to have
second thoughts about using him, but there are no other
volunteers.

February the sixth: B. reacted to S.D. in the expected
fashion. A short time after we had settled him in what he
facetiously calls "the Tank"; checked his respirator and
nutrient drip; and begun to pipe the subliminal "white-

sound" through his ear plugs, he fell asleep: a reaction confirmed as normal by Vernon at Princeton, during his "Black Room" experiments in '54.

February the seventh: B. has been asleep for twenty hours: no doubt as a result of his previous mental exhaustion. "The Tank" is behaving perfectly.

February the fourteenth: B. has now been deprived of sensory contact with the world outside his immersion chamber for nine days. He sees only a diffuse grey blur of light, hears only a constant homogeneous sound. He is aware only of the contact of the water in which he is suspended. The nutrient drip, respirator and pumping mechanism continue to function well.

9 p.m.: B. has begun to make leg movements. They are irregular and correspond roughly to the act of walking.

10 pm.: Using the one-way telephone system, we attempted to contact B. and warn him that his movements were disturbing the drip-feed connection in his arm. There was a pause—during which the leg-movements subsided—before he acknowledged us, using the previously agreed code; one long blink to indicate he had heard.

We then attempted to ascertain the reason for his movements, asking if he had become uncomfortable in any physical way; and if, as a result of this discomfort, he wished the S.D. period to be terminated. His reply was negative. My assistant then asked if he had experienced an hallucination, and attained an emphatic affirmative signal, accompanied by a vigorous nod of the head which threatened to dislodge the electrodes taped to his skull.

We assumed that B. had experienced what Vernon notes as a "Type Three" hallucination, in which the subject perceives definite objects, as opposed to the more common manifestation of vague spots and blurs at the periphery of vision. We were unable to discover the reason for the leg movements which accompanied the hallucination. My assistant advanced the tentative theory that B. had actually *participated* in an hallucinatory activity.

February the eighteenth: B. requested that the experiment be terminated. Two or three weeks will pass before he is fully recovered physically. He is vague when questioned on the subject of his hallucination, which has occurred on an average of twice a day since he first experienced it. He shows no signs of the mental disorder which he exhibited before the experiment: in fact he is unnaturally calm and self-possessed.

March the tenth: B. has disappeared from his studio. Of late, he has been difficult to deal with, remote. I suspect that he regards my presence as an invasion of the private world he has constructed about himself. I am sure that this world has its roots in "the Tank". He is unaware of the danger of complete withdrawal in which he has placed himself. As ever, he sees himself as the Eternal Artist, oppressed by the bugbear of science.

Monad: painting again, her denim legs hypnotic. The canvas is nearly complete; her end product is already an accomplished fact. Bailey: idly following an out-of-focus blue sprite as it dances with a complicated palette. Bailey: living the motorcycle vision of Gossing, who travelled his own perspective too far and too fast.

Bailey had been preoccupied with the problem of the vanishing point for some days before he remembered Gossing.

The first possibility to strike him had been that of his never reaching it, that the hallucination would develop no further. He had defeated that argument somewhat smugly —by refusing to believe his mind uncreative enough to condemn itself indefinitely to vain pursuit: there must be *something* at the end of the road. He began a search for an alternative, coming up with theories ranging from the eventual confrontation of himself by himself, to the achievement of Nirvana. It was during this search that a youthful recollection of Gossing provided him with a prefabricated answer. Gossing's way of death became a fixation of proportions matching those of the vision.

Gossing had died on the road.

He had been engaged in Ph.D. research in applied physics at a northern university : an isolated, withdrawn character who rarely spoke, and segregated himself stringently from campus society. He had evinced no open interest in women —to be fair, he had displayed none where men were concerned, either—and had regarded the antics of the student body with a sour contempt. Experiments with lysergic acid had been the vogue at the time, and these he had reviled with bitter humour, considering them a foolish blunting of the mind as a tool : referring to them scornfully as "Happy attempts at intellectual suicide".

In his last term he had built himself a motorcycle; a low, squat thing that resembled an insect—its dropped handlebars replacing the anhedral wings of a wasp at rest. The machine had been extremely powerful : Bailey could recall only vague detail, but remembered fear and dislike of the thing. He had been interested in it only as a symbol of Gossing's state of mind.

Bailey had concluded that Gossing's lack of sexual life left him with a need to assert somehow his essential maleness : the brute, thrusting power of the motorcycle had confirmed his masculinity. It had also furnished the sense of purpose his leisure time had lacked because of his refusal to participate in the university's social life—which, however inane, provided an imperative diversion.

Gossing had ridden the machine with an aggressive flair; laying it closely and almost viciously into corners—often with the footrests and silencers throwing up sheets of sparks as they grounded on the road surface—as if the road belonged to him alone. But he had not been reckless; every move had been calculated in his dry computer of a brain before being put into operation. There had been a harsh beauty, even poetry, in the way he had handled it; in the way that neither man nor machine had submitted itself to the other, but had remained inseparable parts of a single organism—a high-octane centaur of the clearway.

Towards the end, however, he had become an extension of the thing. It had gained ascendency, almost a personality of its own; and the road had exerted a malign fascination. He had been a pathetic, possessed creature at the time preceding his death; steadily more introverted, driven by the lash of what could only be represented by the hard, unreeling ribbon of the road and the howl of the slipstream; a man doomed and hurling towards an unavoidable, gory climacteric.

Bailey's identification with Gossing was strengthened by the vanishing-point, their common crux. Monad's exotic dance with the palette knife and canvas retreated. Bailey had ridden once—once had been enough to kill the desire— on the pillion behind Gossing, and it was on that one experience that he now based his re-enaction of Gossing's final ride down the Perspective. He gave the word a capital letter impulsively; accepting the identification with Gossing; uniting Gossing's reality with his own vision. The muted hum of traffic outside gave way to a bellow of power. There was a seven-gallon fuel tank between Bailey's knees and fifty brake horse-power surged responsive under his throttle hand. Without a noticeable shift of reality to unreality, Bailey *was* Gossing.

"It's like this: out there, everything's simpler. On the road it all boils down to this: at that speed, you're either going to make it—or you aren't . . ."

Gossing–Bailey straightened the bike up, powering it

63

firmly out of the last leg of the bend. Ahead, the road ran straight as a die, then broke into a series of elbows: the vanishing point. This was the ultimate high: here, for a few cathartic seconds, was the orgasm of the gods. He settled his goggles and flattened himself on the fuel tank, his chin on the foam pad. Deliberately, almost reverently, he wound back the twist-grip.

". . . for a minute, you're on your own, and free: the fear doesn't come until you have to slow the thing down."

Freedom: the road was a great elongated vee, empty but for the single particle of fierce energy that was Gossing–Bailey and the motorcycle. After two miles, the speedometer and the Perspective came together as one image, a circle superimposed on an open compass; the image of fulfilment. Then he had to start closing down.

"You don't want to come off the high. It's hell closing that throttle; it's admitting that neither yourself nor the experience is immortal . . ."

Orgasm is a transient thing. The machine wasn't slowing. In the space of a microsecond there happened an eternity of fear. He managed to nurse it through the first bend at a hundred and ten, taking a resigned pleasure in the achievement. But it was impossible at that speed to pull out and align the machine for the next one. His body jerked in a last ejaculation of panic. There was an improbable silence.

Bailey came back to the studio. Nobody had been sure whether Gossing or the motorcycle had failed on that ultimate straight. He knew now.

Bailey: supine on the studio floor—head pillowed on hands to stop them shaking—watching Monad paint. The choreography of creation is almost complete.

Bailey had not moved for two days. Inertia had finally

taken him: he had found a balance between himself and the city. Only his mind moved, and that with growing lethargy, walking slowly along the Perspective.

Gossing's ghost was laid—or rather, it had taken its place in the schema of Bailey's illusion. Gossing and the circle of the speedo they had fished out of a ditch, still intact, needle wedged by the failure of its mechanism at one hundred and ten miles an hour; Hollis—Empirical Man and his Experiment; Gardner—the city anxiously looking after its own victim: all were integrated, assimilated; subordinate to the vision, and yet the bricks of which it was built. Bailey–Gossing/Hollis–Gardner were a composite entity, running down to the point of absolute rest.

He had ceased to eat and could not remember when he had last relieved himself. The only motion for some time, other than his plodding feet on the Perspective, had been Monad's dance, her choreographic coupling with the easel and canvas: and he sensed that this too was terminating. She was a blue shadow behind a window, the stained-glass screen of illusion. Somehow, hers would be the final act. Monad's was the hand privileged to throw the last switch. He was content to wait. To all intents and purposes, he was still in the womb of the Tank, waiting to be born for the third time . . .

Monad made a last movement, decisively. Bailey, sensing the finality of the motion, tensed; the Perspective faded, but the girl was remote: her actions came across a great gap of space and time, a gulf, a hole in his awareness.

She danced over to him, smiling. He saw her once more as Monad in pale blue, then her identity slipped into the gulf. He felt her kiss his forehead, saw her step back and parody a curtsy, sweepingly. She motioned at the canvas.

For perhaps five minutes, he searched the picture; taking in its greens and greys; noting the sharp, geometrical definition of the skyline, the great tonal vee of the road, the unmentionable vanishing point. This, then, was it.

He conjured back the Perspective and compared the two overlapping images in his field of vision. Then he manipulated them gently, and they came together, matching perfectly, the world on the canvas and the weariness of his mind.

Tiredly, doggedly, he began to walk.

"Do you like it?" said Monad, anxious.

But Bailey could hear only the monochrome wind.

WORM IN THE BUD

by

JOHN RANKINE

*Apart from alien bacteria and viruses, an explora-
tion team investigating an extra-terrestrial world
could well bring back a more insidious and explosive
method of human destruction . . .*

WORM IN THE BUD

PAIN was a memory; non-pain a voluptuary's dream of indulgence.

Prone on a tumbled scree of black basalt, needling everywhichway in polygonal disorder, Quinn faced a cliff-like slab which was familiar. He was still at the site of the R.V. then?

He moved his right hand and brought it round to the front of his visor. It was still there, intact, responsive, able to wiggle its gauntleted fingers at him. Not ground down to a stump as his mind had told him.

He looked at it stupidly. Then let his head fall forward to the stone, hearing the knock of his crystal visor as though it was all happening to someone else a long way off. Vision clouded. Then liquid ran beside his mouth. He was crying.

The miniature power pack on his back began to deliver, and dry, warm air circulated to clear inner surfaces of condensation.

Now it was a dream sequence. Something had happened, but he could not remember what it was. It was fading quickly, receding more definitely as his mind tried to swing out a grapnel and hook it back.

Had he been delirious then and was now sane, or had there indeed been a white operating theatre and faceless golden Chrysaorites taking him apart, filling every sense bud to the threshold of intolerable pain?

In any event there was not much improvement in being

where he was, except *carte blanche* to die in his own time and without pain. The ship would not be back.

As though he had always known that this was his function, the purpose for which he had been created; he knew that he had a mission to fulfil, if and when he did get on board a spacecraft once more.

Where it had come from, he could not say, but knowledge there was, now present in his computer mind, which could be used to manipulate the power pack of any space cruiser to a point of runaway which would turn the craft into an immense bomb. He was orientated at that deep level where a man is as much a stranger in his own mind as any visitor, to carry out a programme.

It would be a consummation. A triumphal end to his own life-span. When the ship homed on the great artificial asteroid which was the nerve centre of the Inter Galactic Organisation, he would know what to do. Freedom would return. The order-keeping authority would be no more.

His captors had done well. They had built on a foundation of idealism and a will to serve humanity. It was in the name of freedom that he was orientated on his saboteur's course.

That it would be licence for a chaos in which only the hatchet men of the Galaxy could thrive was not mentioned. Golden ant-men of Chrysaor, blue-white reptiles of Scotia, all the malcontents and outlaws of the Outer Galactic Alliance would have their field day.

The rock floor appeared to waver beneath him. Swinging surges of black cloud engulfed his mind. He was out again.

When Peter Quinn finally opened his eyes to clear vision, it was morning on Chrysaor and he remembered nothing, not even that he had been dreaming. He only knew that the ship was overdue and that he had waited there a long time. Unless Fletcher brought the ship down in the next twenty-four hours it would be too late.

A similar conclusion had been reached in the small control cabin of the I.G.O. special shuttle *Ishtar*.

Unarmed and travelling on fragile diplomatic immunity, she was used for ferrying negotiators and I.G.O. commissars on the Organisation's endless missions across galactic space. This stint, more delicate than most, had brought her to Chrysaor, cinder-heap home of a marginally hominoid life-form which was a centre pin of the Outer-Galactic Alliance.

Fletcher had been against the move from the first.

Ostensibly he was borrowed from the military fleet to fly a three-man team of diplomats to a negotiating session in Anchiale, the administrative capital of the planet. I.G.O. was falling over backwards to offer peace-keeping contracts and in this instance was hoping to ratify certain commercial links which might be mutually beneficial and would provide a handle to hold the Chrysaorites in a web of self-interest towards keeping the peace.

After years of experience, Commander Dag Fletcher did not believe any agreement could be made to hold.

Utterly alien in modes of thought—particularly in valuation of individual status—there was, he believed, no common ground to tread. High-level perambulating intelligences operating on a group principle. Cultures based on sanctity of individual rights were at a loss. It was as illogical as expecting snakes to make *entente cordiale* with rabbits.

It was the side angle which had reconciled him to the mission.

Ishtar was a very special item indeed and carried some assay gear which would surprise a lot of officials who had checked her in and out of a dozen security-tight spaceports.

Even Chrysaorites could not live in the baking ruin of the equatorial belt of their ancient planet. But there, the distant probing eyes of I.G.O. science had tentatively identified huge deposits of infrangom. If this could be confirmed there was even more need to work out trading treaties with the planet. Mining concessions would have the important functions of bringing out the metal which was vital in spacecraft design and in tying Chrysaor to an alliance of self-interest. This might or might not weaken her bonds with O.G.A. but it could only be good.

Peter Quinn of the I.G.O. survey section had been dropped in an inhospitable region of arid heat with supplies for seven days and an R.V. for the fifth. He was to make a sampling survey of the ground and be ready for *Ishtar* on her return trip to dip briefly and dig him out of it.

Fletcher, fuming and fretting after endless petty hold-ups had lifted off from Anchiale spaceport on the tenth, aware that in the conditions of the terrain Quinn would be fighting a rearguard for mere sanity.

Although he knew the basic enmity of Chrysaorites, he could not put a finger on a definite act which looked like deliberate tactic, but the nudge of a sixth sense told him that much of the delay was deliberate.

Not that any Earthman could tell what went on inside the smooth golden egg heads of the officials. Built on the external skeleton principle of Earth-type insect life, the Chrysaorites had no discernible facial reactions to mirror inner stress. Only actions gave a clue.

When *Ishtar*, pencil-slim with the blue and white I.G.O. emblems glowing at waist and cone, flung herself into a yellow sky, Fletcher reckoned it made no sense. If they were on to the ploy, they would want him to find Quinn dead. Three days without food would not do that.

He began calling out course data in an urgent monotone. Pulling back below escape velocity and setting for a landfall without an exploratory orbit was enough to think about. It was small wonder that I.G.O. Command had brought in a corvette captain for the chore.

Ishtar handled like a flexible missile. Built on corvette lines, added power units and control gear took up the load factor given to armament in the military craft. He was allowing part of his mind to appreciate the fine handling capabilities of the ship when his communications executive, Aline Greer, came up on the general net.

"Communications One to Commander. Z53T19."

A cool voice. She had played it that way ever since he took over the ship. Making it clear that a civilian crew had its professionalism and did not need any help from the military arm for this or any mission.

That and the fact that she had no special use for the lanky, lean-faced commander himself. Peter Quinn, identifiable now as a sprawled, puppet-figure bang on Z53T19, was the lodestar of her compass mind.

Fletcher perversely using civilian procedures said, "Okay, Aline. Good girl. Get a line out. Check me as I go. Manual. Manual. Wait for it, Mortimer. Steady as you go."

Aline Greer had to bite back a protest and then found herself thrown into a situation which was entirely new. With Fletcher taking the ship on manual and playing it with incredibly fast reaction times, she was faced with constantly changing course data which was obsolescent while she checked it back.

Then she got the rhythm of it and met his pattern of effort like an extension of his own mind.

Ishtar fell like an arrow, checked in a blaze of retro and flexed down on hydraulic rams in a local storm of black dust.

Dag Fletcher had time to say, "Hold fast, Communications," in as formal a way as any military exec. would have expected, then he was climbing out of his gimbal-mounted couch on the revolving command island and making for the freight hatch in the base.

External gauges were still showing 50°C. as he went

73

down on the extensor arm of the freight grab to blistered rock which sent shimmering waves of thermal agitation past his visor.

Peter Quinn had struggled to his feet and was swaying like a drunk, still holding a bulging sling pouch of rock samples. Plugging in on his dangling multi-cord, Fletcher said harshly, "Okay, Quinn, you're back in the Navy. Step along this way."

Watchers in *Ishtar* saw them pick a zig-zagging course through needle pinnacles of rock until they disappeared below the bulge of the side. Then the whine of the retracting elevator sounded through the silent ship.

Aline Greer was in the loading bay and got a dusty reception. Visor hinged back to frame a pale oval face with full lips and Epstein eyes; she was all set to break out Quinn's seals and give him a hero's welcome, when Fletcher's voice reached her in a dehumanised snarl from his external speaker.

"Save it, Greer. Why are you out of your couch? Count down as of now. Move."

Hesitation was marginal, blue-green eyes blazed with contempt for a tyrant, then she was climbing up through the hatch with a light brown pony tail swinging emotionally behind her.

She thought, "The mean-minded swine. He knows how it is between Peter and me. He could have waited a few minutes. I know we have to get away. I'm not a child. High and mighty Commander-bloody-Fletcher. Just you wait. That's all. Just you wait. I'll get even, if it's the last thing I do."

She might have been appeased if she had seen Fletcher taking care to strap Quinn into the sickbay couch; using precious seconds to see that he had a drink. So that by the time he was climbing into his own resilient bed, G was

74

already beginning to build and his last moves were made only by momentous, sinew-splitting effort.

Using every milligram of *Ishtar*'s enormous thrust, her commander ran down the equatorial line for a full due before clawing back on to a course.

Other than answer direct calls for navigational data, Aline Greer was silent in mounting anger. So he was content to let Peter Quinn sweat it out after all he'd been through down there. Twice she was on the point of asking to be released to go to the sick bay. Each time a call for her special attention came up and pride held her to the console, though either of the assistant communications men could have handled it.

Finally, with *Ishtar* on a line which the computers could hold, two hours after lift-off, Fletcher was satisfied.

He said on the general net, "Okay Number One. You can wrap it up there. Routine watch. Stand down. Aline, you can go and play Florence Nightingale. Get him on his feet. I want to see him in half an hour."

"Check."

It was a minimum response and bitten off with a clenched teeth sound at that.

"And Aline . . ."

"Commander?"

"Take it easy. There's more involved in this than Quinn's well-being. Or yours. Or mine."

"I understand that."

In the brief exchange she had broken out the twenty-one seals on her suit and stepped out of it in a skin-tight leotard like a delphinium-blue nude from the collapse of a re-union dinner cake. Whatever the state of Quinn's morale she could only do good.

When she released his straps he could not stand and she had to help him with the stud seals, strange and awkward when working in this unfamiliar back-to-front fashion.

Visor off, his face was deathly pale and as his head went limply back on the headrest she saw two tiny red incisions placed symmetrically on either side of his broad throat.

An observant girl, she was sure that they had not been present ten days ago. Some projection from his equipment must have done it, since he couldn't have had his suit off in that frying pan. She smoothed his dark hair back from his forehead and kissed his honourable scars.

Reaction was immediate, but unexpected. Anyone finding Aline Greer hanging over their cot was entitled to a bonus surge of *libido*; but Quinn was galvanised as though by a high-voltage kick.

Hands to his throat he sat straight up. Whatever he was going to yell out died in his voice box. Eyes focused on Aline. He said, "Oh. It's you. Hello then. Where's Fletcher? I should see Fletcher."

It was not the best copy that could have been knocked out to please a ministering angel and an emotionally involved one at that. But it was not the form of words that set Aline back on her heels as though she had been slapped.

Difficult now to believe since it was so fleeting; but the first expression on his face after her lips had touched down, had been one of terror.

She stood up slowly. "I'll go and tell Fletcher. He wanted to see you as soon as you are fit. What is it, Peter? Was it very bad down there?"

He swung his legs off the narrow acceleration couch and hauled himself upright. Now he seemed to be recovering very fast. He said, "Aline, you look good enough to eat. But it'll have to wait. I'll report to Fletcher, then I'll be along to your cabin for a bite. See you."

Then he was moving out and along a narrow companion. From the back, stiff-legged and zombie-like; but near enough to normal for her to leave him to do it all by himself.

76

"So you had trouble with your circulating gear? It looked all right when we picked you up."

"I got it fixed, but it threw me for a day or so. Then when the real pinch came, I guess I folded quicker than you would expect."

"But you got what you went for?"

"Oh, sure. Enough to send the assay unit singing in its cell. It's there all right. Enough infrangom to keep the I.G.O. block happy for a generation. Pure form too. No problem for extraction. But I can't see Chrysaor giving a concession. They use it. I know they have supplies in more accessible regions, but they could easily set it up for work in that area. More easily than anybody else. In fact, don't they have conditioned labour groups which can work without a life support system in anything up to forty-C.?"

"That's not our problem. Now we know, it's a diplomatic matter. You've done well. I'm sorry we had to leave you down there. One hold back after another. I thought at one time it was deliberate. Just holding us because they knew we had a man to pick up. You saw nothing of them?"

"No, I saw nothing of them."

Fletcher looked closely at Quinn's eyes. Must be tired, of course. Wanting to tell all to la Greer, too, no doubt. He had a sense that Quinn was keeping something back. But what could there be? Anyway, that again was an I.G.O. problem. If they wanted to probe into the why and wherefore they had the time and the means. As of now, he had one task, to get *Ishtar* to base in the shortest possible time. Then he could get back to his corvette and let the politicians get on with it.

Seven days rationalised time and *Ishtar's* computers threaded their double string to home on the wandering artificial asteroid which was the I.G.O. nerve centre.

Quinn, seemingly fully recovered, was back at his console as second man in power.

Aline Greer, who shared a watch with him, was looking more thoughtful with every passing day. With their objective a visible glowing speck on the main scanner, she was finally pushed to overt comment.

As the watch detail changed and she handed over to her second man, Quinn, a quick mover, came behind her. "I'll lay on some food, what would you like?"

"Don't worry about me, Peter. You go on. I'll be down in a few minutes."

"All right. See you." A brief patronising tap on the crown of her head and he was gone.

Dexter, the co-pilot and navigator for the watch detail, had finished his transfer to Navigation One and was gathering small items of gear from the locker below his console. Aline Greer said, "Chuck? A word in your ear. Can you spare me a minute?"

"For you, anything." Chuck Dexter took her arm and piloted her into the admin. centre next hatch down the corridor. Everybody wanted to touch, she thought, it was no great catch to be comely.

"What is it, then? Tell your uncle all."

Dexter, a short chubby type with a round cherub's face and small strong hands, radiated far more than average thermal glow and she could feel warmth coming her way. A living negation of the old crack about unaided machines not being able to pass on heat at higher temperature. It took an effort to get her mind off the second law and her plunge into confidence was abrupt.

"It's about Peter Quinn."

"What's he been doing to you, then? Or not been doing as the case may be."

"Seriously, Chuck. There's something queer about him, since that experience on Chrysaor."

"Bound to be. He had a bad passage. Take him a bit to forget it. Probably thought he'd bought it. Brings you up with a jerk a thing like that. He's probably looking hard at life. Is lechery all?"

She moved impatiently to the door. "I can see you don't want to know."

"Have you spoken to Fletcher?"

"No. He wouldn't understand either."

"Look, Aline, I don't think there's anything wrong with Quinn that a week's leave won't put right. But if you've gone off him, say no more. Talk to me instead. If you have any serious worries on a stability count, you'll have to tell Fletcher. Okay?"

In the servo, they were halfway through their meal when the ceiling tell-tale came up with an amber alert. Fletcher's voice added its commentary. The new watch must have routed him out almost at once.

He said, "Unidentified craft coming up on parallel course. Stand by for an All Stations call. You have about five minutes. Out."

Quinn went very still and the girl, ultra-sensitive where he was concerned, said, "What is it, Peter?"

"Nothing. Unusual that though. Chances of meeting up with another craft must be very small."

It was such a well-known fact that it was odd to hear an experienced crewman give it a form of words.

"So?"

"Nothing. Just that I don't want any delay."

"What difference can an hour make in rationalised time? Even if we change course to take a look."

Dexter said, "Fletcher won't change course. This isn't a corvette. We only have speed as a safety factor. If there's any doubt he'll be away for slates."

The tannoy blared again to make a period and give his diagnosis the lie direct.

Fletcher's voice again, incisive, moving them from the servo in a dive for gear, "Action. All personnel to stations. Major course change."

Dag Fletcher, swinging easily on the command island turntable looked along the grey hulk of a space derelict. Dexter checking back through the current identification manual said, "Sorry, Commander, no joy. Whatever it is was obsolete a long time ago."

"That figures. I've seen nothing like it."

Ishtar, pulled back by deceleration which mounted as much G as a primary lift-off, was keeping station fifty metres from the stranger. Every head in the command cabin was turned to look at it. Massive cylinder; a hundred metres of it on a thirty-metre diameter; pear-shaped nose cone with a spiky frill of antennae below the bulge.

It was turning slowly. A massive entry port like a barn door came into view with a tangle of lines drifting out from an inset hitching rail. Then the name *Bayev* in metre-high lettering.

Fletcher said, "Grabs away, Number One. Lay us alongside that port."

While Dexter was setting it up, he talked in basic speech, to the senior I.G.O. Commissar in *Ishtar*'s v.i.p. suite.

"Commissar, this is a major space hazard. I have to go aboard and make a report. Delay will be minimal."

Enliarri-Ba used the same tonal shorthand. He had difficulty with all Earth languages, "Very well, Commander; but be brief."

Grabs held and the mass of the derelict worked its logic, *Ishtar* began to circle round her with lines pulling taut.

Coming up against *Bayev*'s side was like standing at the foot of a wall. Fletcher was reminded of a rundown wharf with empty freight sheds, an intangible air of menace. Inside there was an impression of great space.

Dexter said, "She was never blasted off a pad. Assembled in space, this baby. Something to be said for it. You could do a square dance in this recep."

Fletcher was checking for biological hazards and came up with a clear reading. There was no trace of occupation. It looked as though she had gone on her long voyage without a crew.

Not having to lift this bulk off a planetary surface, her power pack was ludicrously small compared with *Ishtar*'s. A whispering iodine beam motor pushed out enough urge to navigate by. Power One, a lean raw-boned Scot, sat at the power console on an observation and control deck which would house thirty astronauts, he said, "It's my opinion that this gear's still very serviceable. For what good reason would any crew leave a ship like this?"

It was a question which had already occurred to Fletcher and he could not answer it. One thing was for sure, *Bayev* should not be allowed to carry on alone. Whatever fantastic journey she had done, some quirk of forces had redirected her to the major shipping lanes of the galaxy. An I.G.O. engineer detail would have to supervise her destruction. Disperse her in gas that would not harm the hurrying ships.

It was too big a unit to search in the time he had. Somewhere in the unfamiliar control panels, there could be an auto log which would tell all. Somebody else could find it. He said, "We'll take her on a course for H.Q., then drop clear and make our planetfall. I.G.O. can send out the disposal boys to pick her up. Aline? Did you get that? Shove it out straight away to I.G.O. They'll probably have us on a plot anyway."

He waited five seconds thinking about the spaciousness of the big ship, debating whether the universal practice of making craft powered for their own take-off was indeed a right decision. There was no answer from *Ishtar*. He said again, "Aline. Do you read me?"

Aline Greer's voice came up as an etliolated whisper on the general net, but there was enough of it to communicate its harmonic of frantic appeal. "Using emergency power. Return to base. Commander, Power Two has sealed himself in the power module. Controls to command centre all dis. Do you read me?"

Even in the emergency, she could not bring herself to put the blame on Peter Quinn by name.

After the derelict, it was like coming into the world of men from an afternoon in a mausoleum to return to *Ishtar*, pencil slim, vibrating with life.

Aline Greer, as senior rank left in the control cabin, was still against reason working through check procedures to isolate faults. Only small local power sources were available. It was when she had sent a moving human operator, as in the days of steam, to take a look below, that she had found it impossible.

Fletcher wasted no time going through the drill. Plugged in as extensions on the same ring circuit, he spoke directly to Quinn's suit intercom. "Quinn, what goes on down there?"

For a long count of four there was no reply. Quinn's operational role was to man the auxiliary console, set in the confined spaces of the power pack itself. Normally it had no function. It was there as an insurance policy for the unlikely event of some major blow-out at the nerve centre. A subsidiary cortex.

When his voice came up, he sounded infinitely tired; but determined in a way that brooked no argument. "I have brought every command circuit to this board. The course is set. I shall home on H.Q. You cannot stop me and you cannot warn port management."

"Warn? What's this 'warn'? They already have us on the beam. We're expected."

"We are not expected to crash land with the pile on a runaway."

It was said with a flat finality that carried conviction. He had hit on some adjustment to defy the centuries of engineering development which had gone to make the power packs fail-safe.

"Look, Quinn. Whatever it is that's got into you, think again. Destroying I.G.O. H.Q. will set back Galactic progress for a century. Hold fast on that and talk it out."

"I have no more to say." The click of a relay made a period. He had opted out by throwing away his ear trumpet.

Fletcher said, "Mac, how long before you can dig him out of there?"

"God knows. Thickest seal on the ship. Half a metre of infrangom. Designed to shield the forward hull from anything short of a nuclear blast. Cutting gear's in the lazarette. He's sitting on that, the wee bastard."

Dexter said, "So now we know what was on his mind, Aline."

She made no reply; but Fletcher said, "Did you have reason to think he was under strain?"

"I thought he was not fully recovered after the mission on Chrysaor."

"You know you should have reported that to me?"

"Yes."

Out of the direct vision port there was a shift in the angle of the flexible grab lines.

Dexter said, "He's giving it the gun. Using course data already in the pipeline. He can't lose."

"What time have we got?" Dag Fletcher settled himself at his dead console.

"Under eighteen hours." Aline Greer read from the last workout on her pad.

"Due to go down at 22.47 precisely."

"Okay. Then it's simple. We transfer to the derelict. There's equipment there. Make it good. Raise them on the distress beam. They can send up a corvette to destroy *Ishtar* before she can make it home."

"What about Peter Quinn?"

"Worry about yourself, Aline. If you can't make the signal, we all buy it. If you can, we have to cut loose and go on a tangential course with nothing between us and infinity. No tracking gear in the galaxy will find *Bayev* again. She's already been lost for a century or two. You're working for humanity's good, not yours."

From *Bayev*'s observation deck *Ishtar* was a dark, hurrying outrigger. A shadow moving across a star map. Fletcher was no nearer any solution of the problem set by the empty ship. Only a fully equipped engineering section could hope to sort out its mechanical detail and find an auto log if there was one.

Eleven crew and three political supercargo sat or stood or walked about the great observatory, set like a horseshoe gallery above the well of the command centre. On the factory floor, Aline Greer and her communications team worked from first principles among a litter of dismantled electronic gear.

Ignoring personal safety they had stripped off their protective suits. Fletcher with visor hinged back leaned over the dividing rail. "How long, Aline?"

It was typical of him that he did not mention the time she had taken or what was left to go.

There was in fact no need, she had been watching the clock for twelve hours.

She pushed a swathe of damp hair from her forehead and

walked over to stand below him, looking up. Slim arms hanging straight by her sides, pale oval face with dark rings of fatigue adding brilliance to her eyes. "When's the deadline?"

"Not long now."

"How long?"

"Half an hour at the most. After that he's near enough to blast the asteroid whatever they do."

"I can't do it."

She put out her hands to the bottom rail of the barrier and held on as though to stop herself from falling. In spite of his clumsy gear, he vaulted the top bar and dropped down beside her.

"Nobody could have done more. I've seen what you were doing. The only sure way. You had to do that and nobody else could help."

"There's one thing though."

"What's that?"

"It's honestly only just occurred to me. The last figures I fed into the course plot were for *Ishtar*."

"So?"

"Weight, power, all the usual data."

He thought she had worked herself into a stupor and was talking for its own sake. He gathered her hands from the rail and led her out of the pit to a chair on the upper deck.

Then the force of it struck him before she could go on.

Ishtar alone was one thing. Chained to *Bayev* she was another, with a different set of handling characteristics. A plot, set up to take her in, would be wildly out for the combined mass. Already they would be marginally off course for the asteroid. The deviation would grow with every kilometre.

He said, "You're a doll. You've got all the time in the world to fix that gear." Then he was calling for Dexter.

85

"Get across to *Ishtar*, Number One. Bring out as much food as you can break out in fifteen minutes. We're cutting loose."

They saw Quinn from the oval port of his narrow cell watch incuriously as they ferried the bundles across. Once he waved as though he did not greatly care, so long as he could complete his mission. Then they were ready to cast off.

Aline Greer went out to try an appeal in mime, like a fish from a neighbour aquarium. When he recognised her, he turned away and refused to look.

Back on board *Bayev*, she said, "What has happened to him?"

Fletcher said, "Something more than just exposure. Those delays at Anchiale begin to smell. He could have been pressured."

"Peter would never go over."

"Not consciously. But it can be engineered. A man's truth has many facets. The past, fossilised on his profile and his present are only two aspects of it. What he will do in the future is not fixed by either. Particularly if psycho manipulators take a hand."

"That means we are all contemptible."

"Not contemptible, vulnerable. Whatever the truth of that, there is work for you. Get something working here or we're in this derelict for a life term."

"Like its crew. Perhaps they had a chance to bale out and took it."

"Maybe. Maybe we shall never know. Get on with that transmitter. Just enough to make a homing signal. All right?"

Aline Greer walked to the broad shallow stairway that led off the observation deck, a trim, erect figure; delphinium blue nude descending a staircase. Conscious of his eyes watching her she stopped on the highest tread and half

86

turned to look back. His eyes were serious with no unseasonable, ulterior design. She said, "I'll do what I can."

In forty minutes by *Bayev*'s ornate chronometer, she was checking home the last stage of a communications plant which would raise Earth planet. She took the console herself back in the anonymity of her space suit and called Fletcher formally on the intercom, "Communications One to Commander. All systems Go. Calling I.G.O. control now."

Fletcher said in the same impersonal key. "Thank you, Communications. Get me Military Control."

Ishtar was a brilliant arrow diverging now from its target in *Bayev*'s huge zoom scanner by a quarter million kilometres.

Dexter said, "Quinn must know now that he can't make it. What will he do? He can't navigate *Ishtar* for any other planetfall."

"He won't try to." Fletcher was answering Dexter, but speaking to Aline Greer. "He was programmed in some way to make that bid. Now that he's failed he'll be back on his own motivation. He'll try to make *Ishtar* fail safe."

Before she could speak, the arrow had blossomed into a white asterisk. When the brief brilliance burned out there was an empty screen.

Fletcher said, "He knew what he was doing. He knew there was something in his mind which he could never alter, so he has destroyed it. I'll log that for his record. Nothing contemptible there, Aline."

Dexter was returning. From the satellite, a bright, thumbnail sphere, two needle flecks of light were streaking out. He said, "They're on their way. You did well, Aline."

But she was no longer there. She was standing with Fletcher by the huge oval viewing port. In direct vision, the satellite was lost in the vast star map.

She said unexpectedly, "The sad thing is that what I feel

now will pass. He was a good man, but legitimate grief is no more lasting than anything else. Isn't that a terrible thing?"

Dag Fletcher said, "To understand that is the beginning of wisdom. Within the framework of self limits you make your own truth."

He put his arm round her shoulders, an incongruous, clumsy embrace of pachyderms; but it carried a psychological comfort and they stood together looking out until the moving particles which were the searching corvettes had separated into discreet and eager shapes.

THEY SHALL REAP

by

DAVID ROME

The closed environment story usually applies to a situation where Man has to take his natural conditions with him in order to survive. Australian author David Rome, however, shows that it could well apply to a normal community right here on Earth.

THEY SHALL REAP

WE pulled up under the big red-on-white sign that said: RICH VALLEY DEVELOPMENT CO. and sat in silence for a moment. Outside, the sunlight was slanting over the mountains in cool yellow shafts. But in the car we were in serious mood. Even the kids.

"Well," I said at last. "Everybody sure this is what we want?"

In grave voices, the kids said it was. And Eve met my eyes and nodded quickly. Her eyes were big and soft and she looked like she might cry at any second.

"Our own farm, Adam."

"It'll be hard work."

"We'll never have the chance again. Not at this price. Not at half the price."

"Still, all our money will be in there. No backing out. You know what the agreement says—we stay, or forfeit our purchase price."

"They're giving people such a wonderful chance," Eve said. "People like us. You can't blame them for trying to discourage the sort who might not stay. Rich Valley ..." Eve said softly, looking down the misty green V of country beyond the building which contained the Development Company offices. The sun rested like a cool steel disc on the high mountains in the west. It began to melt and run across darkening slopes towards us.

"Come on," I said. "This is where the Rice family belongs."

The kids were out of the car before I finished the words.

Pete led Trisha, his voice a wild whoop that sharded on the grey-green mountain slopes. She followed more sedately, dark hair loose and heavy on her thirteen-year-old shoulders.

"Pete will have room to run out here," I said, pressing Eve's hand. "Really run. Like the little savage he is."

She smiled happily and nodded. We stopped as the kids waited impatiently for us, looked down the valley again. Smoke from the settlements spaced along the valley sent thin spirals up against the purpling sky. Peace. Room to breathe.

"We're lucky, Adam," Eve murmured. "Lucky to have the chance."

"Well, we passed the tests. They wanted us to come."

"And all the others living down there, they'll be people like us, Adam. People who believe in kindness and goodness."

"They'll be good people, honey. It'll be a good place to bring up the children."

Trisha's big grey eyes were watching us in the gathering dusk. We smiled and she smiled back. Pete danced on one foot and waved to us to hurry.

All of a sudden lights came on in the Rich Valley Development offices. Warm and welcoming lights.

We sat in a semi-circle around Judge Whymore's desk while he completed the agreements. Judge Whymore had told us on our first visit to Rich Valley that he didn't act as a judge any longer.

He and four others, who had owned the whole of the valley between them, had founded the Development Company. Their aim, he had told us, had been to build a community of people who were looking for escape, escape from violent cities and the seething pressures of suburban life. People who coveted tranquillity.

We had taken a written psychology test and an exhaustive—and for Eve and Trisha embarrassing—medical examination as the first steps towards securing one of the two hundred farms in Rich Valley.

I suspected that ours had been a borderline case, the balance weighed by Eve and Trisha, both creatures of inner peace and self-containment.

I considered myself honest and practical, too honest and practical to succeed in a business world of dishonest contracts and speculation. But my streak of rebellion had been inherited by Pete, neither of us completely tamed by the angelic women of our family.

"You're extremely fortunate," Judge Whymore told us. "You are our final family."

His broad and happy face beamed at us.

"You're all prepared?"

I nodded. "House sold, furniture too. Just clothes and a few personal things in the car there."

"We will make our clothes in the valley," the Judge smiled. "But, of course, you will want your own things for a while."

He rose, tall and twinkling-eyed.

"I'll drive down with you. Help you settle in."

"Thank you," Eve said.

He smiled and placed his hand on the soft darkness of Trisha's hair. "Thank you, Mrs. Rice."

We drove down the dark and winding road which led to the valley farms. In the oblong of my mirror I watched the yellow lights of Judge Whymore's car following us.

The mountains seemed to bend down over us from the silver-mercury sky. Lights pinpricked the darkness of the foothills every mile or so.

Judge Whymore's car rushed past us and his tail-lights flared as he slowed and showed us the turn off.

A half mile later, we drew to a stop outside the farm-house. Our farmhouse.

93

Lights were burning and the front door was open, spilling molten gold into the night. Figures appeared and loomed closer as I shut off the engine and Trisha and Pete tumbled in excitement from the car.

I stepped out and hands clapped themselves into mine and I saw smiles and happy faces in the sheen of light.

"Our last family," Judge Whymore was saying. "Isn't it wonderful?"

"And two children," a woman's gentle voice said. "Two sweet children. Isn't that wonderful too?"

We all trooped inside and the owners of the faces became neighbours. Five in all. I remembered no names, but their pleasure at having us here was real and soon I felt that I'd known these people all my life.

Everyone carried something from the car. Judge Whymore insisted on carrying Yellow Bird's covered cage inside, planting it in the centre of the big cherrywood kitchen table and then taking off the cover so that everyone could see Yellow Bird blinking himself awake.

"What is it?" someone said, coming closer.

"Canary bird," Judge Whymore said, and suddenly there was sadness in his voice. "A beauty too. Whistler, I'll be bound."

"Oh, dear," someone said softly.

They all looked at us with unhappy faces.

"What's wrong?" I asked.

"Nothing. No, nothing at all," Judge Whymore said, covering Yellow Bird's cage. Then his eyes twinkled again and darted around the room. "Where are those children of yours? Now where are they?"

Pete's face appeared in the doorway. "I just looked out a window and saw someone," he announced.

Judge Whymore stepped forward, one eyebrow arching upward.

"Saw someone?"

94

"Yes, saw someone watching me. From the edge of the woods. A lady."

Judge Whymore laughed. "A lady would come right on in and introduce herself." He looked at the open front door and everyone else looked too. "She isn't going to come," he said in a few moments.

"Pete," I said. "It's dark outside. How could you see anyone?"

"Moon's up," he said. "Big as a silver dollar. And she had a dog with her."

"Dog?" Judge Whymore's voice was sharp. "There are no dogs in the valley, boy. You imagined it."

"Didn't," Pete said. "That dog was the biggest I ever saw."

"That's enough, Pete," I said. "Go and find Trisha and bring her down here."

"Trisha's outside, looking at the moon," Pete said, and smiled.

We all walked to the door. The moon lay big and cold on the tops of the trees of our woods. Trisha's silhouette was pressed against its face. A breeze came and lifted her hair like slow dark wings.

"Trisha!" I called, and she turned and came towards us.

"Beautiful child," someone murmured.

"Obedient too," Judge Whymore said.

We soon settled in to life in the valley. Found out our neighbours' names and then discovered that we had two hundred families as neighbours and it would take six months to learn them all. There wasn't a day when someone didn't drop in to make us feel at home.

Sheldon Ward was our immediate neighbour to the south. He had been a banker in Baltimore until he saw the Rich Valley Development ad. He had been one of the first to move into the valley with his family. His farm was prospering.

"They all prosper," he confided to me one night. "Every last one. No blight, no green fly, no black fly, no aphis, no apple sucker, no Big Bud, no red spider. Before I came to the valley, Adam, I studied farming chemistry. Potash, phosphates, nitrates to enrich the soil. Know what we put in the soil here? Crops."

Sheldon was right. On the slope facing east I planted and staked apple trees in the rich deep loam. As a windbreak I close-planted damsons and I filled the sunlit sheltered folds of countryside with Louise Bonne and Conference pears and peach bushes that came to fruit with astonishing speed.

The days were sunlit and long, the nights cool and long. School in the valley began at eight and ended at four and it was after five by the time Pete and Trisha appeared plodding through sweet smelling dust on the road below our house.

Trisha didn't mind the long school hours. But Pete grew more rebellious as the days moved on.

"I'm tired of being in a class on my own," he said.

"A class on your own?" I tousled his hair. "Now come on, young man. You're neither so bright or so stupid that you need that kind of attention."

"Well, almost on my own," Pete insisted. "Just the three of us."

"Three? Are you serious?"

He nodded a vigorous ten-year-old head.

"Just three of us."

I walked over to the pump and began drawing cool green water up from the earth. "Pete, there were thirty or more in your class when you started at the school. I took you there on your first day. I saw them."

He stayed in the house shade, watching me.

96

"What happened to the others, Pete?" I said. "Did they just vanish one day?"

"We took tests," Pete said. "I guess I kept failing. Everyone else passed and they went up a class."

"Except three of you?"

"Yes."

The bucket was brimming full. I scooped a dipper full and drank the dark sweet water. "Pete," I said gently, "you were always up there with the others in your last school, before we came to the valley. What happened?"

He hung his head and then shrugged. "Guess I'm good enough at reading and writing and arithmetic. But not the other things."

"What other things, Pete?"

He lifted his eyes. "Just things."

Eve appeared in the doorway behind Pete, her pregnancy great and still surprising in front of her. There hadn't been any signs, but it must have begun before we came to the valley, because suddenly she was bursting full and happy at the prospect of some fresh-born crying around the house.

"Adam!" she called.

My eyes held Pete's a moment more and I said, "We'll see about those tests. I'll come to the school with you tomorrow."

"Adam!" Eve called more urgently.

I went over to her. "It's Yellow Bird," she said.

She led me inside. Yellow Bird's cage hung by the open window. In the dusk I could see the cage rocking and swaying, hear the panicky flutter of wings.

"What's wrong with him, Adam?"

"I don't know. He acts like he's scared to death."

We watched the bird. He seemed to be trying to get out of his cage. He beat his wings against the bars until a yellow downy carpet covered the window-sill and drifted

97

to the floor. His tiny eyes were bright as flames as he dashed himself again and again against the bars.

"Let him out!" It was Trisha who spoke behind us and we turned, startled. Her own grey eyes were huge and wounded with pity.

"Let him out," she whispered.

I opened the cage door. Yellow Bird launched himself like an arrow across the dark room.

His small beak slashed at Trisha's face and then he swerved and banged into the white stone wall and fell to the floor.

Trisha bent to the small warm bundle.

"Poor Yellow Bird," she said. And blood shone on her cheek.

Eve turned on her side and the bed creaked softly. "Aren't you being foolish, Adam? Really, aren't you?"

"Eve, I went to that school today. I saw it with my own eyes. Three children in a classroom meant for ten times that."

"Room, Adam. They need room. For the new children."

"That's another thing. All these babies due. Doesn't that seem strange to you?"

"Babies? Strange?"

She sighed and sat up. I saw the glint of her hair in the moonlight that was sliding through our bedroom window.

"Tell me what's worrying you?"

"Eve, they act like Pete is some kind of savage."

"You called him a savage yourself once," Eve said gently.

"He's a cub, Eve, just a sharp-toothed eager cub. But these tests the kids are given. They say he fails them all. These people act as though he's actually evil——"

"These people? We're part of 'these people', Adam."

"Do we belong here, Eve?"

"Yes." She lay down and buried her cheek into the white pillow. "Yes."

"I wonder."

"Don't wonder, Adam. If this valley is a strange place then it's wonderful too. I have the feeling that if we doubt it, it can all disappear. And never have been. I'm afraid of that happening. So afraid."

Her hand moved to mine and pressed. "Don't ask questions, Adam. For my sake don't ask them."

"Honey, I have to——"

"You have to belong, Adam. We all have to belong. Trisha already does. Can't you see that in her face? I've never seen her look more beautiful or be more quietly attentive to whatever she's doing. Composure and peace. I feel them too. And I'm happy that our new child will be born here. You and Pete must learn——"

"Pete says he won't go back to school."

"He'll go back. We'll make him go back. It's important to all of us that he goes back."

"He can have a couple of days at home, give him time to think it over."

"No," Eve said gently. "He's behind already. He can't afford to miss his lessons."

Eve closed her eyes and soon I heard the rhythm of her breathing change. Moonlight shone on her face and on the full white mound where the summer sheet curved over her stomach.

I lay awake. I listened to the creaking and settling of the house around us. I thought of the laden apple trees and peach trees and the rich valley soil. I remembered how Judge Whymore had taken the cover from Yellow Bird's cage and shaken his head sadly. I thought of the glint of blood on Trisha's white cheek.

Something flapped wildly outside the bedroom window. For an instant, sitting bolt upright, I saw the gleam of

99

yellow eyes and the cruel curve of beak. Then the vast night bird was gone, whatever it had been, planing away over yellow acres of meadows and woods with a screech.

I stood at the window and looked down towards the edge of the woods. In the glow of moonlight I tried to separate light from shadow, real from unreal. And then I was sure. I could see her poised there, bent forward as she watched the house. By her side was the dog Pete had described to us once.

The dog lifted its snout to the silver sky and howled. The note rose until it trembled from the mountains and filled the night with its call. I heard Eve start awake.

"Adam, what is it?"

Suddenly I pressed my face to the cool glass. I stared unbelieving at the small figure darting from the house below me and making swiftly across the grass towards the woods.

Once, he looked back. He might have seen my white face at the black window.

But he turned and ran on. The girl and the dog came to meet him.

"Pete!" My lips broke against the pale glass. "Pete!"

I went up into the woods after him. As I climbed through the sword-shadows, roots and earth underfoot, the moon began to set.

A single shaft of red light gleamed between the trees and I heard the low growl of an animal ahead. The sound brought my arm hairs prickling erect.

She stood beside the softly snarling animal, one hand fondling its ears. She looked about eighteen years old, her hair long and blonde, face an oval of shadow. She wore blue jeans and a thin black sweater and her feet were bare.

The growling of the animal went on as I faced them. I

could see its fiery eyes and the glint of white teeth. Its ears were erect, its coat harsh and black in the last light of the moon.

"A wolf?" I said wonderingly.

"The Wolf, mister." Her voice was low and lilting with the sound of the woods and countryside. "They kilt 'em all, all but General. He was a cub an' I nursed him. Now he'll eat out your throat if I say."

"Where's Pete?" I said softly.

"Your boy? Pete's a fine boy. He's safe."

"Where is he?"

The wolf growled. "I cain't tell you," the girl said.

I clenched my fists and unclenched them. The moon had gone. The woods were black, the figures indistinct and unreal.

"Who are you?"

"M'name's Ruth. Ruth Kitel."

"Ruth, listen to me. Do you know what is happening here in the valley?"

"Dumb Brother knows. But he cain't tell. Cain't tell me 'cause I cain't talk with my mind. General knows. Dumb Brother told General . . ."

"Who is Dumb Brother?"

"What I told you. My dumb brother. I guess his name is Josh."

"Where can I find Josh?"

"You find Dumb Brother and y'find your boy."

"Where?"

"Cain't tell."

I stepped angrily forward. The wolf growled a low warning and the girl put her hand on its ruff.

"Take it real easy, mister."

"Ruth," I said softly, "what are you doing up here? You—and Josh—and General. What are you hiding out here in the woods for?"

"Not just three of us," she said. "There's more. Lot more. And now Pete."

"Pete can't stay."

"That's f'r Pete to say."

"He's just a boy!"

The wolf growled. She said softly, "I got to go, mister. Done try t'follow me, or General will feed off you."

"Ruth, why do you want Pete?"

"Pete is the one who wants us, mister."

"You said there were others, others besides you and Dumb Brother. Who are the others? Where are they?"

"Who?" she said. "Where?" She laughed softly. "Why, they all aroun' you now. They bin watchin' you all this time. Didn't you see?"

Something clattered in the brush behind me and I whirled. Small eyes stared out at me, then blinked to darkness. There was a woosh and a roar of wings overhead and two flights of birds banked like bombers over the tree tops, black crosses against the starglow.

Ruth was moving away, fading too.

"Ruth!" I called. "You wanted me to see you tonight! You sent that bird to draw me to the window. You knew I'd follow Pete into the woods."

She turned and said softly, "I didn't send the bird, mister. I cain't do that. Only Dumb Brother can speak to the wild creatures."

"You wanted to see me. Why?"

"I tole Dumb Brother you might be one of us. I said of all the people in the valley, you and Pete might belong here in the woods."

"Perhaps I do. Take me to Dumb Brother, let me talk to him."

"Can you talk with y'mind?"

"I don't understand."

"Then you cain't."

"I'm coming back, Ruth. I'll be armed. Or I'll have the police with me. I'll be coming for Pete."

"No gun in the valley, mister. No police neither."

"I'll go outside the valley."

"You cain't," she said. "They won't let you."

"Won't let me?"

"Try it. You'll see. Ain't no way any of us can leave this valley."

The lights were blazing in our house. Eve and Trisha sat in straight-backed chairs in the kitchen. When I entered the room Trisha went to the hot plate and poured steaming coffee.

Trisha's eyes were big and soft. "He's run off," she said.

I nodded, then glanced at Eve.

"He's gone. I couldn't find him. He must be hiding out in the woods."

Trisha brought me coffee. "That's where he belongs. In the woods."

I looked into her grey eyes and saw a screen come over them.

"He's a little savage," she said, turning away.

Outside, night breeze moved through lush apple crop and nibbled at the golden peach orbs. Rich soil lay black in furrows ready for more planting and folding, more growth. I watched my daughter move around the room. She wore a white nightdress over her own growing young body, midnight hair sweeping her shoulders. Her lips were pale and faintly smiling. Her cheeks were flushed with health, eyes clear and gently happy.

"Why?" I said softly.

Trisha's warm back was turned to me.

"Why is Pete a savage?" I said.

"He just is, I guess. He was just born that way."

"No one called him a savage when we lived outside the valley, Trisha."

"Outside the valley?" Her voice was low and blurred with wonder. "That was forever ago."

"Pete was good at his lessons then."

"Yes." Trisha's head nodded gravely.

"But not now?"

"The lessons are different now. Pete won't try. He doesn't belong here." Trisha turned and her eyes rested on mine.

"Am I a savage too, Trisha?"

Eve was watching us intently. Trisha nodded slowly. "Yes, Mr. Andersen says you might be."

"He's your teacher, isn't he, Trisha?"

"Yes."

"He teaches all of you. All you children. All except a few like Pete. And in a few months there'll be more children for him to teach. What will he teach them, Trisha?"

"The new children won't need teaching."

"Did Mr. Andersen tell you that?"

"Yes. He said we're to be kind and gentle to the new children when they come."

"Isn't it dangerous to be too kind, too gentle?"

"I don't understand."

"The turtles we saw at Pennekamp Reef last year. Do you remember them, Trisha?"

She nodded slowly.

"They're protected there, Trisha. But in other places the turtles are hunted for their shells, or their flesh. A giant turtle might weigh hundreds of pounds and be able to carry a man on its back. But do you know what the hunters do? They turn the turtles on their backs. And the turtle is helpless then. But it's still protected by its shell. It can draw in its head and tail and legs. The hunters crack its shell open, Trisha. Under that hard casing the turtle is soft and vulnerable. Its beak is toothless and its body soft. There's no way it can save itself, once its shell is split open——"

Trisha shook her head. "We're not turtles."

"Aren't we, Trisha? Isn't it possible that all of us, here in the valley, are being turned on our backs and having our shells cracked open?"

"Adam, are you serious?" Eve was looking at me with incredulous eyes.

"Something strange is going on here," I said. "More than strange. The crops grow and come to fruit and our children are growing and becoming as golden and tender and helpless as those peaches on our trees, Eve! Suddenly every woman in the valley is having a child! Suddenly Yellow Bird beats out his brains on the wall. Suddenly our son, an absolutely normal and intelligent boy back home, is branded as a savage——"

"What are you afraid of, Daddy?" Trish said abruptly.

"Afraid?"

"Do you think that Mr. Andersen and Judge Whymore and the others have some sinister purpose in making this valley a paradise?" Her voice was gentle and mocking.

"Who are they, Trisha?" I said. "What do we really know about them?"

"They owned the valley. They gave it to us."

"There are other people living in the valley, Trisha. Or there were. A girl called Ruth Kitel. And her brother. They lived here too. Now they're hiding in the woods."

"Hiding? From us?" She laughed softly.

"Hiding from something."

"Adam," Eve said sharply. "When did you find out about these people?"

"Tonight."

"You mean Pete is up there with these——"

"Savages," Trisha said.

Judge Whymore's home stood in a cluster of trees on a knoll overlooking the Rich River. The night wind soughed gently through the top leaves and scratched branches against the star-specked shield of sky. The river was a fat black artery coiling below.

I drew the car to a halt and switched off the lights. I sat a moment, watching the house. It was in darkness. I glanced at my watch and the radium hands showed two in the morning. I snicked down the catch and opened the door and slid out and closed it again.

The front door of Judge Whymore's house was open.

The patch of lighter shadow became the turn of a cheek. One eye was a distant pool of darkness. The triangle of whiteness was Judge Whymore's dress shirt.

"Adam?" His voice carried to me softly.

I walked closer and Judge Whymore came to meet me. His eyes twinkled and shone, his smile glinted.

"I couldn't go to bed yet," he said. "Such a beautiful night. I was taking a breath of this wine we call air."

His dark and mellow suit smelled of cigar smoke and pleasurable evenings with friends. He put one hand on my arm and guided me towards the house.

"Mr. Andersen and the others, we old valley people, still like to get together now and then. But everyone has gone now. How about a nightcap?"

"I wanted to talk to you," I said.

"I know," Judge Whymore said. "And I to you, for a long time now, Adam."

We sat in the big study of the fine old house, Judge Whymore's eyes sparkling and flashing, brandy pooled in his glass like laughter.

"Oh, my, that boy of yours is a problem."

"He never was a problem outside the valley."

"Of course, of course, but our little community is rather special, Adam. You know that. You know it better than most. Adam and Eve. That influenced me, you know. Call me foolish, romantic, but it did." Judge Whymore leaned forward, eyes glistening with humour. "Oh, that boy of yours. What a problem."

"They often are. Have you had children of your own, Judge?"

"Children?" The glistening eyes held mine. "Children? Oh, no, Adam. Never."

"What about Andersen, the teacher. Does he have——"

"Not Andersen either."

"The others?"

"None of us has children," Judge Whymore said. "None of us has a wife."

I raised my glass and sipped from it, watching him over its rim. "Five wealthy bachelors. It was generous to share your valley with us. This project must have cost a great deal of money."

"Well, yes, but it will have been worth it, Adam."

"Worth it? Do you really think so, Judge?"

"Of course." Judge Whymore rose to his feet and went to the window. He moved one hand and the curtains drew back, letting in the darkness. "Why not?"

"You've made people happy, Judge. But how long can it last? I mean, how long can the valley support the people you've brought here, and their children, and——"

"The valley will support them. Believe me, Adam, this will be a paradise."

"For us?"

The twinkle had gone from the eyes. "What do you mean, Adam?"

"The people you brought here are like rich soil, Judge. When the crop comes, the soil has no choice but to bear it."

"The crop?"

"Who are the farmers, Judge? You or us?"

There was a glitter of metal in Judge Whymore's fist. "How intelligent and how stupid you people can be."

"So I was right."

"Yes, you were right."

"You're not human."

"We are human. These are not our shapes. But we are human." The small gun in Judge Whymore's fist caught the light and gleamed. "We came so far, Adam, to your earth. We chose this valley——"

"But people fought you. Ruth Kitel and Josh."

"Dumb Brother. He is a telepath, able to communicate with animals. He instils hate in them, hate for us. But he will not stop us. We brought our soil here. Your people are the soil. Our seed was planted so simply—do you remember the medical examination you all submitted to? Precious seed, Adam, brought through sterile miles of space, from the world where our own people were dying. And soon it will crop. Your people will live peacefully with ours, until——"

"Until we die, and you take over."

"We are not murderers, Adam. Not fiends. We had the power to take your planet. All we took was one valley——"

"This valley, how can you preserve it? What's to stop outsiders from coming in and——"

"No one can come in. Or go out. Ever again."

I sprang. The alien weapon spat a searing cold flame past my face. The heel of my hand hit Judge Whymore's chin and hurled him violently backward. The weapon spun from his hand and tinkled into one corner of the room. I whirled and ran from the room, ran from the house, into the cool press of starlight.

The car started at the first twist of the ignition key. I accelerated in reverse as Judge Whymore appeared in the doorway of the house. The gun in his hand hurled freezing flame again. I spun the wheel and skidded down the dusty road winding from the knoll.

The river swept past as I turned left and picked up speed, making for home. Words spun in huge and silent fragments through my mind.

No one can come in. Or go out. Ever again.

Eve was standing in the starlight, in the wash of my headlights as I swung into the yard. But I could see the small windows of darkness, the same darkness that belonged to Whymore and the others, in her eyes. And the house behind her was too still, too watchful.

I stopped and we looked at each other through the pale windscreen.

"Adam." Her lips made the words. "Come to us."

Trisha stepped from the house. She walked with gentle eyes and womanly grace towards us. And, quite suddenly, I saw the ripeness of her belly under the soft white nightdress. Swelling pregnant ripeness.

Eve and Trisha.

Lost to me.

I gunned the car and spun the wheel and in the oblong of my mirror I saw their figures receding from me. Before I dipped over the final hill and out of sight I saw others join them. My neighbours.

My headlights cut tunnels in the night. I followed the road south through the valley, between the high mountains. Soon I came to the place where the road ended.

It did not end in any way I can describe. There was no wall, no gulf cleaved in the valley floor. It did not peter out or run abruptly into dense forest. I'm not sure if the road ended at all. Or whether, in my mind, there had come an ending instead.

There just was no place to go outside of the valley.

So I reversed the car and drove down into thick brush at

the side of the road and carefully killed my lights and switched off the engine.

I stepped out and for a moment held the ignition key between my fingers. Then I hurled it away. I heard it tinkle to silence in the starlit brush.

A low growl carried to me.

Rustling and chittering began in the brush around me. Yellow eyes watched. Birds hopped from branch to branch, intently curious.

The black wolf emerged a few strides away from me. Ruth Kitel was at its side.

"You came," she said.

"We can fight them. You, me, Pete and Dumb Brother."

Her head shook. Her hand fell to fondle the black wolf's neck. "General will lead the army."

"General——?"

"This cain't be man's fight any more."

THE LAST TIME AROUND

by

ARTHUR SELLINGS

There have been many fascinating stories concerning the apparent paradox of subjective and objective time, but none quite so poignant or explanatory as the one Arthur Sellings presents here.

THE LAST TIME AROUND

He signalled return twelve lightyears out, on attaining peak velocity. Earth station computers—when they finally got his message—would punch out his arrival time to within forty-eight hours of accuracy. They integrated it from the signal shape and by a kind of parallax. The warping of the continuum about a craft travelling near the speed of light gave it a double image.

It took the computers a week to check and double-check. Then the tape went into the traffic banks to start re-scheduling local flights up to six months ahead, to leave the field—and space—clear for his arrival. His ship would "reappear" well outside the ecliptic; all the same, a D.C.P. —direct continuum propulsion—ship demanded a lot of room—and got it.

He came in out of permanent night into the transitory night of his home planet. But Sheppard Field was brighter than day. The lights dimmed as he grounded. They always did. It had become a kind of salute. In fact, it was more of a publicity gesture by the company, to allow full sight of the strange fires that played round a deep-space ship at landing.

They were fading as, ground procedures completed, he opened up and descended, and the battery of lights leapt up to full strength again. Faces were a white blur beyond the perimeter fence. The faint, faraway noise could have been cheering. Probably was.

Reporters clustered. Uniformed field guards kept them back to allow passage to a crewcut figure, who approached with the pumping stride of a little man determined to show that he could walk as fast as a big man. And by implication do anything else. He thrust out a hand. Cameras clicked and rolled.

"Grant?"

Grant smiled inwardly at the query in the voice. But they were strangers, after all, he and this man in a mauve suit.

"I'm Bassick, Chief of Flight Programming. Have a good trip?"

"Good?" Grant allowed himself a smile now. "That depends on what your analysts make of the data I brought back. Quantity's there, at least. There wasn't much room left in the banks by the time I'd finished."

Bassick nodded happily.

"There are also some physical specimens you may find interesting."

"Artifacts?" The corners of Bassick's mouth went down a fraction as Grant shook his head.

"Mineral stuff, mostly. Little life at all. Surprisingly little. A pleasant enough planet as they go. Everything seemed right for a pretty rich ecology, and it wasn't there. But I clocked in full data on that point."

"Well, even negatives can be useful to somebody." The little man turned to the reporters. "Okay, boys, you've seen him. And you've had the company handout. Give the guy a break, eh? He's been travelling fourteen years getting here." A laugh went up. The joke wasn't as familiar to them, a new generation, as it was to Grant. "Press conference tomorrow as arranged, at fifteen hundred hours."

They dispersed good-humouredly enough, photographers taking a few more pictures as Bassick ushered Grant to the Personnel Block.

"A car was laid on," said Bassick. "But I thought you'd like to get your planet-legs."

He used a spaceman's words with the self-conscious unctuousness of the earthbound. Grant decided that he didn't like Bassick overmuch—nor care one whit for that fact.

"What happened to Goodman?"

The other looked up at him with no more than a company man's mask of regret. "He passed on eleven years ago. Heart. They rushed him to Replacement, of course, but the new one didn't take. I was at his side. I don't think he wanted it to, somehow."

That was more than likely, Grant thought. Goodman had always prided himself on his physical fitness. An independent man in a world increasingly dependent on artificial aids. Betrayed by one body, he wouldn't have wanted to start relying on another.

"I thought his son was in line to take over from him. Young . . . Paul, wasn't it?"

"He was. I had more executive points. He left the company. He's with some inner-planet outfit now, I believe."

"And my . . . buddies?" Grant spoke the word ironically. One he had never met; the other he had not seen since training days, two hundred years—Earth time—ago.

"Kroll's doing fine. Hazlitt was grounded after his last trip. His replacement's a youngster called Ebsen. Pity about Hazlitt. Only had one trip to go. But he's making out. Took a farm in Brazil." They walked along a way. "Do you have any plans?"

"What—in case I flunk *my* medical?"

"It's your last time around, too. But I didn't mean that. You look in good shape. I meant, after your last mission?"

"Time enough to think about that. But I don't see myself farming—in Brazil or anywhere else." Grant's face creased in a sardonic smile. "Might buy a small space line and do a spot of hiring and firing myself."

But, despite his joking, he felt a twinge of unworthy fear as they entered Personnel. A truncated service term made a huge difference to a man's finances. That was something you couldn't insure against. With the vast investment the company put into a D.C.P. ship and its pilot—and the timespan between that and any yield—the payment structure was logical enough, with its penalty clauses for failure to stay the course.

It made this life, inevitably, a gamble. Not, ironically, out there—instrumentation took a lot of the risk out of that—but here, in what a man came back to. When he had started out, there had been wry jokes about whether there would be *any*thing to come back to. Star flight had come at the crux of man's technological ability to destroy himself and his planet. But things had settled down over the past two centuries. At every return the world seemed crazier on the surface, but saner underneath, where it mattered.

He felt annoyed to be thinking about the money angle. It hadn't been the money that had attracted him. It needed more complicated reasons to lead a man into a career like this—to giving up the central years of his life to an existence without continuity, isolated from everybody else ... by time, more than by space. The *wish* for that was something the company psychiatrists delved very deep to find in a man. When they did, he was out before he started. They looked for an idealist of sorts, a special kind of loner. A special kind, but there were enough around. The need for perfect physical fitness winnowed the ranks down. A doctorate in science gained early enough to enable an applicant to complete a stringent and specialised training programme by the time he was twenty-five, was another qualification that reduced the number to hardly more than the company required. Which was two when he had started.

Even now there were only three ships. It was an expensive business for a company to be in. And it could be an expensive business for a man coming out into a world of normal time into an unknowable future.

A few inner-planet men, in their midnight blue, were

spread around the reception lounge. They looked up from their drinks at sight of Grant's sage-green uniform; some waved in wary greeting. In their glances was the usual mixture—it didn't change with the generations—of . . . it was difficult to analyse . . . something of envy, something of "You're welcome, Jack," something of resentment . . . and a large amount of workaday relief with the D.C.P. ship berthed, that they could now get back into their own backyard of space.

Grant waved briefly in return—theirs was a camaraderie he could never be part of—and trod the familiar way to the Medical Section. They were lined up and waiting for him.

He came out two hours later, with a clean bill of health, with no need to claim the second opinion which, with everything at stake, was his right. Bassick was waiting outside.

"I've booked you a suite at the 'Venus'."

"What's that? Sounds like a high-class cathouse. What's wrong with the 'Universe'?"

"They pulled it down twenty years ago to make way for a freefall drome. The 'Venus' is the latest and best in town." Bassick's hand twitched at his crewcut. "The other service you . . . ah, mentioned in passing . . . is also available. That's supposed to be the best in town, too."

Grant grimaced. Goodman had been much more pleasantly direct and had brought out a selection, in assorted sizes and colours, direct to the field.

"That's something you have to get back into the habit of. All I want at this moment is a meal of real food, a bottle of real booze, and a real bed. To myself."

An hour before the press conference they had the parade in his suite. The usual train of facts and figures, stereo films, commentaries snipped from a hundred news items and documentaries—and models showing off the current fashions in clothes and ornament.

The Sahara reclamation scheme was now completed. The trans-Australia monorail had been opened. A third generation had been born in Costeaupolis under the Mediterranean, including one child with what some excited scientists said were embryonic gills and others said were just accidents. A man had descended into the Red Spot of Jupiter and come out alive.

The interest in organ replacement seemed unabated since last time, despite the fact that it only afforded a marginal extension of the normal life-span. It simply made sure that most people attained it. This time the ultimate seemed to have been accomplished with an operation on an Indonesian billionaire; his failure to survive by more than six months had been ascribed to over-excitement rather than to anything more organic.

Humanoid robots on a commercial basis were just around the corner. They'd been round the same corner thirty years before.

Skirts, if they could be called that, were back to the length—or shortness—of the twenty-one fifties. Worn with garters, which looked hideous to Grant's eyes. The effect wasn't improved when one model switched on a miniature radio in hers.

But he did his best to be polite to the reporters who were ushered in on the dot of fifteen hundred hours. It was a routine that seemed to be wearing thin to him, but the company called it good public relations . . .

Yes, he thought the current fashions for women were very feminine. He liked the style of mauve suits for men, but didn't intend to buy one this leave. He had enough clothes. Some of them might look rather antique, but he could always find something in the wardrobe like this—he gestured down to his dark jacket and slacks—that fitted in well enough.

Yes, he thought robots might well be just around the corner. Did he think they would ever replace men on spaceships? They might, but he didn't see it personally. A spaceship was ninety-nine per cent robot now, if not in humanoid shape. But it still needed a man to control, to initiate, to improvise.

He couldn't pass comment on the gills—it wasn't his specialty. A primitive race he had encountered on Proxima Centauri Two had seemed to be in process of giving up the struggle on land and returning to an aquatic life. But that had been nearly two hundred years ago. The same old stale joke. The same stock laughter . . .

It was like—the thought came to him, not for the first time—being a visitor to a foreign country.

"This was your seventh trip, Captain. The next one makes up the number, doesn't it?"

"Well yes. Not the number; it's the term that counts—twenty years. The trips get longer most of the time as we push out the frontiers. My successor will either make fewer trips or sign for a longer term." (He turned to Bassick, who flighted his palms in a non-committal gesture.)

"Will there ever be true frontiers out there, men colonising?" He answered a loyal company yes to that, though sometimes he had doubts. "But probably not in your lifetime. Nor even in mine." The same laughter, a bit forced this time, the resentment of the time-bound against this strange élite of men who spanned centuries. But how many of them, given the choice, would make the same one he had, two hundred years ago?

"No, I don't know yet where my last assignment will be to. After I retire? I haven't decided. An inner planet? I doubt it. My plans for this leave? Family? No, I have no family." (Which wasn't quite true, he confessed to himself with a pang, but as true as it mattered.) "Nor home town; that was inundated in a reservoir scheme a century ago. No, I shall just loaf around, try to catch up with the world. Any more questions?"

There weren't.

As they got up to leave, a familiar figure entered, even in a dark purple suit recognisable immediately. No such company manoeuvres as took place in Deep Space Incorporated plagued the firm of Vandeleer and Vandeleer. Grant shook hands.

"The eighth?" he enquired politely.

"The ninth."

Grant smiled ruefully. "The memory must be slipping."

"Not at all. I'm afraid Dad died. Tragically. He was only twenty-eight. The Transworld Clipper collided with a freighter over the Caucasus."

"I'm very sorry. And sorry I never knew him. I should have realised. I thought you looked rather young."

"I try not to." Richard Vandeleer IX laughed. "Your portfolio has given me a few premature grey hairs these past three years."

The room was empty now, the last to leave Bassick, ushering out the drinks trolley.

"How come?"

"Well, first there was devaluation."

"Devaluation? Against what? I thought we had an integrated world currency now."

"Against gold. Integration brought its problems. They had to have *some* standard."

"Seems a bit primitive in this day and age. Did I lose much?"

The other grinned. "I may have got pitchforked into this at a tender age, but it's in the Vandeleer blood. I had a hunch and bought Eurasian Gold Preferred three months before the switch. You *made* money out of it. It wasn't so easy with the tax revisions they brought in just after. They were intended to rationalise the tax position of inner planet people. Some were being faced with double taxation. It blew up in a freak case of somebody getting loaded with *quadruple* demands—for fifty per cent more tax than he was earning.

"I won't go into technicalities, but the revision would have meant that you would have lost all your tax allowances here, without gaining them anywhere else. I don't want to overplay my efforts, but it was tough going. When the machine puts things right for a minority of fifty thousand, it doesn't want to be bothered with amendments to accommodate an even smaller minority of three."

"Especially," Grant commented, "if said minority is rarely home at election times."

"Exactly. It took lobbying and a degree of . . ." He gestured equivocally with one hand.

"Graft?"

"Call it programming. Rather expensive programming. Getting the right questions put at the right time in the right places. I was ready to fight it up to World Supreme Court level if necessary, but that would have been even more expensive and time-consuming. I managed to straighten it out my way, but only just in time for your return."

He drew out a folder of papers from his briefcase.

"Despite that expense, you finished half a million up on thirty-two years ago. In real terms, taking into account the inevitable cost-of-living rise, you're seventeen point two five points ahead. Not a lot, I'm afraid, over that period, but in view of——"

Grant waved away his apologies. "You've done well. I'm satisfied."

The other was young enough to show his relief. "There are some papers here for you to sign." He held out a pen. Grant signed without reading them. He trusted the firm of

Vandeleer. He waited for the last paper to be handed over. Richard held it back.

"And this one ... I should have told you earlier." He looked awkward. "I can handle the financial angles. But I'm still callow at personal details. This is a receipt for the estate of your only grandson. He—he died five years ago, without issue."

"I never expected *him* to have issue." Grant laughed hollowly. "If that's the right pronoun. Estate, you say?"

"Only a few hundred dollars after expenses."

"That's something out of the affair, anyway." He caught the look of embarrassment on the boy's face. He was a member of a tight-knit dynasty, in which family hatreds must be taboo. "I'm sorry. I've no right to be bitter. It was my fault. Have no fear, I shan't repeat the mistake."

A mistake ... *that* was an understatement! It had been on the leave between his fourth and fifth trips, and he still couldn't understand what had possessed him. There had always been enough women. He was under no illusion about his looks; knew that to most women he was only an experience. A strange, enigmatic being, pupils burned black in eyes honed white, hair bleached almost as white against the deep tan that outer space radiation imprinted. A freakish and meretricious attraction, he knew and it was better that way. The experience over, most women passed on, asking nothing in return.

There were the gold-diggers, of course, attracted by the news items about the wealth of D.C.P. men. But gold-diggers employed lawyers, who soon dug out the fact that the wealth was more potential than real. The penalty clauses made sure of that, with the company having first lien upon the lion's share until the day when his service was completed and the discharge papers signed. More to the point, no amount of scheming could separate the money from a man who was going to outlive you, anyway.

Helen had come in neither category. Yes, she had been undemanding—but making the more demands on him for that, because she had been helplessly in love with him. She had woken in him the worst thing possible for a man in his position—a sense of responsibility to another. Resisting it, he had tried to rationalise it into a conviction that he loved her in return. They had married in a village in the Catskills.

A week later the company cabled him notice of his next assignment. A long trip—longer than any he had made up to then, or since. A company decision, born of boardroom conferences and balance sheets and time factors, had sent him out for forty years.

He had come back to a Helen of sixty-seven, with a son whom she had tried pitifully to model after his father, cramming him to qualify in the same business. The son had had three breakdowns; at forty he was a sad creature, older in all fact than his father, painting tenth-rate pictures in an attempt to justify his living on the fund that Grant had set up for his wife.

That would have been supportable. No man could be sure of his progeny. It had been far worse with Helen.

He had been prepared for her ageing; prepared loyally to do all that he could to make her happy, to make amends for the unnatural existence to which he had condemned her. He had *not* been prepared for a Helen determined crazily to pretend that time had stood still. A Helen who had used every artifice of twenty-second-century cosmetic surgeons, who *paraded* before him to entice him, in the grotesque negligées of a world foreign to him.

It was that—the contradiction in her craving to turn the clock back, yet needing the sustainment of the latest fashions in order to feel young—that symbolised the un-bridgeable gulf between them. *That*, more than the old body behind the cosmetic façade, the mincing, imploring gestures, that sent him fleeing from her.

The long mistake was over, then. But he winced in pain at the memory of it, and felt like an executioner as he signed the document.

He sighed heavily. "Well, if that's all the business, let's go downstairs and have a drink. You *are* old enough to drink, aren't you?"

Richard Vandeleer the Ninth looked up from zipping his case. "Try me."

Two large drinks later, Grant felt no better. The surroundings didn't help, the fluorescent patterns changing and swirling over the walls of the huge bar. They might be the latest thing in decoration, but they weren't restful to eyes that had not had the decades to get used to them.

But it wasn't the present that disturbed him . . . and he wasn't sure whether it was the past or future which did. In thirty, forty years—of Earth-time; two or three of his own—he would be back on Earth permanently. The comparison that had entered his head at the press conference—that he was a stranger in a foreign country—returned to him. One could spend a few months' holiday in a foreign country and be diverted by its different customs, the strange language.

But to settle there?

He drained his drink. There was an answer to the feeling, if not to the final problem—the old answer of inoculation, a smaller dose of the larger disease. He snapped his fingers to a waiter. The man came running.

"A gazeteer," Grant told him.

The man blinked. "I'm sorry, sir. If that's some kind of a new drink . . . or an old one, I'm afraid I . . . oh, a *gazeteer?*"

Grant nodded. "A world one."

"I'm not sure if the hotel has one, sir."

Grant held up a hundred-dollar bill. "Find one."

It arrived inside five minutes, looking and smelling

straight from the bookstore as Grant opened it at random. He stabbed a blind finger to the page.

"Biarritz. Department of the Basse-Pyrenees. Historic resort, made fashionable by the English in the nineteenth century. Population . . ."

He looked up at Richard.

Richard gazed at him for a long moment, with a sympathy beyond his years. "I'll arrange the flight. And a good hotel." He drained his own drink. "All a part of the service."

"You're a true Vandeleer," Grant told him quietly. "One small request, though." The walls were flaming orange now. "Make it a *small* hotel."

Two weeks in the French town did much to restore his spirits. Heaven knew where Richard had found the hotel, *L'Auberge Basque*. It was surely too small to be listed in any travel guide; a family affair of a dozen rooms, a zinc-topped bar and a small restaurant. The owner, M. Vidal, was a lean man who smoked black French cigarettes in a holder which he carried at a jaunty angle. He discarded it at intervals to serve—and help consume—meals which belied his ascetic lines.

The inn was typical of the town. In an international world it still retained an essentially French flavour. In itself one of the first of the international resorts—some of the old buildings still bore English names—the tide had swept over it and on. Few skyscrapers had encroached here.

It was September, and he was less noticeable—less *different*—here in a place where everybody was deeply tanned. Resort clothes seemed never to change much; they didn't jar the eye like the bizarre fashions of New York. He spent his days strolling by the yellow sands, watching the breakers coming in; occasionally, as the mood took him, going out to ride on them. His evenings he spent sipping drinks on the terrace of one café or another, listening to velvet-panted French kids strum out ancient French songs on guitars. He found his palate adapting to the same acrid cigarettes whose scent was part of the air of the place, to aniseed-flavoured Pernod.

It was a peaceful life, the peak of its excitement a modest flutter at the roulette tables of the casino. The greater gamble that was his life, his future, became more and more remote every day. Until . . .

He came back to the inn for dinner and had to pass her table to reach his own. The tables were set close in the tiny restaurant. He said, *"Excusez-moi, madame,"* in his poor French, then, such was his uncertainty with the language and its manners, added a suffix of -*oiselle*, making grotesque the simple word.

The gold-haloed head turned. Amber eyes looked up at him. Red lips parted in a warm smile. *"Je vous en prie,"* she said.

In the bar after dinner, there was only one stool vacant, and it was next to hers. He said *"C'est libre?"* and she answered, "You're welcome." The words were American, but the accent was unmistakably English.

It happened as simply as that. As fatally simple.

Her name was Etta—Etta Waring. An ancestor of hers had written a diary of life here in the days before the First World War. She herself had just finished an international congress in Barcelona and had driven across here out of curiosity. She was an anthropologist, a doctor.

He told her that he was a doctor, too, of physical science. And she said, "Reminds me of the story by . . . Thurber, was it? . . . one of the classical humourists . . . no, Leacock. He was a doctor of literature. Aboard ship, a blonde ricked an ankle and the call went out for a doctor. Leacock rushed to her cabin, but found that a doctor of divinity had beaten him by a short head."

They laughed together and the danger point—talk of their occupations—was past, without his having had to reveal—or conceal—the exact nature of his work.

They went surfing, or planing over the calmer waters of St. Jean-de-Luz along the coast, or just lazed by the old port of Bayonne, watching the fishermen unload their immemorial freight. They were days made rich by simple pleasures.

One of them they drove, in her replica E-Type Jaguar, up into the Pyrenees, to the places of cold waterfalls and ancient villages. They stayed in one village, in an inn even tinier than the *Auberge Basque*, a room quaint with carved beams.

And he knew then, with a dreadful certainty, that he had come full circle ... back to bitter memories, of mountains humbler than these, of a village less ancient, an inn ...

And this time threatened to be even more bitter, for now it was heartbreakingly sweet—and this time it was mutual. At breakfast he knew that he had to tell her. At what should have been a time of quiet intimacy, of few words, over *croissants* and wild cherry conserve and coffee, he had to introduce the shockingly incongruous subject of his work.

He pushed his plate aside and, early as it was, ordered cognac. Etta's eyebrows rose, but she did not demur. He tried to settle himself, but the words still came out hopelessly awkward.

"You know ... who I am? My job, I mean? You don't ..."

She smiled gently. "What, read the popular magazines? No, hardly at all. I didn't know who you were. I do now. I wrote home to my people—to tell them about you. I hope you don't mind. They told me. They recognised you from the name and description I gave them of you."

"And they disapproved?"

"Disapproved? Why ever should they?" She smiled again. "I'm a big girl, anyway. I'm thirty-three."

"Thirty-three," he said, his face strange. "Yes, you told me. But you don't know the whole of it, obviously, or you wouldn't talk about it so calmly."

"What—the subjective time factor? Yes."

"But you can't know the full implications. For us. Unless . . . you do feel the same way I do, don't you?"

"Do you have to ask?"

"That's all we seem to be doing—asking questions. There's no answer, you know."

"Every question has an answer."

"You, a scientist, can say that?"

"*Because* I'm a scientist—yes. In time."

"Don't mention *that* word again." He tried to smile, with little success.

"Couldn't I go along with you this last trip? With my scientific training, I——"

"You'd be payload. Anthropology is the least required subject—the least profitable line."

"Profitable? I thought it was a government project. You mean it's a commercial thing?"

"So far it is. There are no dividends for any government in it yet. Inner-planet traffic *is* a government-backed thing. There are still remnants of military thinking behind that, of national advantage. There isn't, of course, but the blocs are committed to it. At a considerable loss. Every assembly in the world has a strong anti-space lobby. No government that values its survival could afford to take the risk in deep space yet."

It was a relief to talk about impersonal things for a moment.

"For Deep Space Incorporated it's a long-term project. So long-term, and needing so many billions of capital, that they're the only firm in the business so far—after two

128

hundred years. They sell the knowledge we bring back—to research foundations, other companies—but that doesn't pay for half of it. They're gambling on being the first in the field, with perfected techniques, in readiness for the day when it really opens up out there. *If* it opens up. It's a big gamble.

"What we do is to extend those techniques—and our knowledge of deep space—system by system. If one of us found a civilisation out there comparable to ours, things would open up, in a heck of a hurry. Everybody knows now that that was the whole impetus behind man's hunger to get to the planets—to find a companion race, a touchstone. Even the remains of one. But they didn't. Nor have we among the nearer stars. Just a few primitive species. Valuable to the biologists, but nothing developed enough to be of interest to your field——"

He was swinging back to *them* now. And it could be deferred no longer.

"*I'm* payload enough. Every item of expenditure is costed down to a cent. The pay isn't huge—by objective time standards. It just piles up while I'm away. But even I couldn't afford to commission a passenger—even you."

"Couldn't you pull out now?"

"I *could*." He told her, briefly, about the penalty clauses. "It would mean coming out with a few thousand dollars— to start all over again on."

"Money's not that important. I have money, anyway."

"No—the money's not important. And it's not the main factor in all this. Completing my mission is. I wouldn't call myself a company man . . . companies seem pretty small things out there in space . . . but I dedicated myself to this job. I have to go through with it, to the end."

"I understand," she said quietly. "Neither could I give up my work . . . even for us."

"In your case it wouldn't be the same either-or choice.

129

There could be a compromise. There's no compromise in this." He smacked fist into palm, impotently. "Why should this have had to happen *now*! The last time around."

She laid a hand on his. "It's hard—terribly hard. I've known for three days. I knew it would make difficulties. I haven't let it spoil things."

"You didn't know the full facts."

"I knew enough. I won't let it spoil things now."

"Then you can accept it, accept ... us ... as something transient?"

"It doesn't have to be. You'll be away ... how long? Twenty, thirty years. I'm prepared——"

"No. *No!* I tried that once. It doesn't work. It *couldn't* work."

He got up and paced the little room. The sun, moving between peaks, sent a sudden shaft through the unshuttered windows, drowning the room in light.

She got up and came to his side, her hair a golden haze.

"Then we'll just *have* to accept it," she said quietly.

"Easy words."

"I know, my darling. Easy and shockingly inadequate. But what more can we say? Or do? We'll have memories. Hell, why do the simplest and truest things always sound so corny? But we *will* have. And we can——" She stopped abruptly. "How much longer have we got?"

"Three, four weeks. At least"—the thought impinged—"*I* have."

"Then so have I. A new academic year starts soon, but the University can do without me for that long. And I the University." Her tone was flippant, but her look, as she gazed at him, was one of utter tenderness.

"*God!*" He took her in his arms, and she was trembling. "I've always been glad to get back into space. Every time I've felt more and more of a stranger on Earth. This time it's going to seem very lonely out there." He laughed sadly.

130

"*It's a fine and private place, but none I think do there embrace.*"

"That's not quite what the poet said."

"I know. He said the grave. That's one place where all rates of time become equal. The *only* one."

"Let's not get morbid." She kissed him once and long. "We've still got a lot of living to do. Let's get back to the big city."

But she was abstracted, saying not a word unless she were prompted and then only answering in monosyllables, all the way back to town, driving along the narrow mountain roads like an automaton.

When they got back, he found a cable waiting for him. He was sure she noticed—sure she guessed what it was—but she made no comment. Up in his room he opened it. He did a simple sum, made even simpler by practice. He would be away for thirty-four years of Earth time. Two and a half of his own. It could have been worse. But when he came back—for the last time—he would be forty-five. Etta would be sixty-seven. Exactly the same age that Helen had been . . .

The next morning he was up before eight. He knocked on her door. There was no answer. He shrugged; early as it was, she must have gone down to breakfast before him. He went down, to the table they had shared ever since that first night . . . and she was not there either. Only an envelope with his name on it.

He felt suddenly empty. He pulled the curtains back. Her car was gone from the tiny, gravelled parking lot. He brought himself to open the envelope.

Beloved,

I've taken the dawn flight to London. I don't know just how long I'll be. No more than two weeks, I hope. Dreadfully sorry to cut into our time—that bloody word again!—like this, but it's for a good cause, believe me. I can't tell you any more until I get back—and perhaps not even then, if this doesn't work.

Don't pick up any blonde English anthropologists while I'm away. Or anyone else! And *please*—wait for me, beloved.

Etta.

The crippled days dragged along. He drank more Pernods than usual, spent more time at the casino, found that he could not face the sea. Its emptiness was too much an image of the lack in his life.

Twelve days later she reappeared, as abruptly as she had left. Her car was back in the lot and she was waiting for him at their table when he came in for dinner.

They looked at each other for a moment. Then she was out of her chair and in his arms, saying, "Darling ... darling." The French in the dining-room smiled as the French have always smiled at lovers, tolerantly, sympathetically, the old nostalgically.

"We can't talk here," he told her. "Have you eaten?"

She shook her head. "I couldn't."

"Nor could I, now." He led her on to the terrace. Somebody brought out glasses and a bottle of Pernod. Grant poured the drinks, watching them turn to milk as he added ice and water. He brought his eyes up at length to hers.

"I've decided .. no, I couldn't bring myself to do that ... I'm ready to let you decide. If you say so, I'll go back on my contract. I've had a lot of time to think it over while you've been away. The company won't lose *that* badly. They'll have a reserve pilot ready. I——"

She shook her head slowly, halting his words.

"That's something I wouldn't hear of. I wouldn't before and I won't now. Besides, darling, it's too late."

"Too *late*? What's happened? Why did you leave for London in such a hurry?"

"To have an illegal operation." She spoke the words coolly.

"A—*what*!"

"Well, not illegal exactly. Not yet sanctioned. It's a new technique, with all kinds of social problems involved. You know the way we English always worry about the social problems. The whole thing only took five days, from the start to the final checks to prove that it had taken. But I had to spend the best part of a week inducing the doctors to do it."

"*Please*—don't keep darting around the subject like this. *Operation*? What operation? What have you had done to yourself?"

"You make it sound like something dreadful." She smiled. "And sad. It wasn't, because of my motive in having it done, though I suppose it could be." The smile became wry. "The ward was a fine and private place, but none I think did there embrace. They see the process as having most use in perpetuating intelligence. It's ironical, really, that it should have been used in this case to serve the cause of lovers."

"For heaven's sake! Your blasted English coolness!"

"It's not easy to tell. Briefly—I've arranged that you will find me waiting for you when you come back, unchanged by the years."

Appalled, his mind lurched back to Helen and *her* pitiful attempts to defeat time and its passing. "You can't! I've had my assignment through. I'll be away for thirty-four years."

Her smile became enigmatic as she made a pretence of counting on her fingers. "Fine. It'll be a slightly younger Etta waiting for you. By a few months."

"What's happened to you! I thought I knew you. When

did this sadistic streak creep in?" His voice was baffled, rather than bitter.

"I'm sorry, darling, really I am. I'm not being sadistic. Just a little shy. I'll have to come out with it . . . I'm going to have a baby."

"*You're——!*"

"Don't be appalled. Just listen carefully while I say it again. *I'm going to have a baby.*"

"But——"

"I told you it was a new technique. Do I have to go into the details?" She sighed. "I suppose I do have.

"Well, it's not really a new technique; only for humans. It was first done back in the nineteen sixties, by an Oxford team led by a Dr. Gurdon, with . . . if I have to bring them into this . . . frogs. They found that if they transplanted the nucleus of an ordinary body cell into an egg half-killed by radiation—its own nucleus killed—the egg developed just like a fertilised one. The cell and the egg from the same creature. They've only recently discovered how to do the same thing successfully to a human being. Now do you see?"

His mental defences, overwhelmed, would not allow him to see it. He listened dazedly as she went on:

"I told you that you will find me waiting for you. You will. It will be *me*—exactly the same. Even to the name. I'll christen her Etta too, naturally. And don't worry about it being anything else but a girl. That presents no difficulty these days, with this or any other birth."

Light filtered through, then suddenly it was blinding.

"But—it *won't* be you. To me it will be, but——"

"But that's all that matters. We can't both of us meet again, but this way one of us can." She laughed, but she was close to tears, he knew. "If you see what I mean. It can come true for one of us."

"I—I can't find the words."

"Don't try, my darling."

"I *must*. I feel selfish—more selfish than I could have believed a man could feel. You went away and did . . . this . . . and while you were gone I couldn't even come to a decision, except to leave it to you to decide. I feel the worst kind of a——"

She put a finger to his lips.

"No, my dear, you're not the worst kind of anything. You're the best kind of something very special. And you're not selfish. Society is selfish in demanding what it has from you, without even recognising the extent of your sacrifice. Except——"

"No," he said. "You can't use that word for me after what you've done. *Yours* was the sacrifice. I'm not——"

"*Please*—let me go on. I insist. Except by treating you as some kind of a freak. I had plenty of time, in the ward, to catch up on the popular papers. Plenty of time to realise just what it must have been like for you. That only sustained me in my decision. I'm glad to have done it—glad with all my heart. So please don't protest any more. It was the only way—and it was a happy chance that there *was* this way, and that I knew about it and was in a position to argue my way through to taking it."

"But . . . I won't protest . . . but how do you know that she'll even like me? One sacrifice is enough. You can't condemn a child to growing up to a foreordained point in her life, and then . . . it's a terrible compulsion to impose on a human being."

She smiled, but her lips trembled as she did so.

"It won't be a compulsion, beloved, but a dream to live for. A realisation. She will have the advantage on me. I didn't know, living my years out, just what I was waiting for. She will. And she will fall in love with you, just as I did. Because she'll be *me*. Not an ordinary child, with all the genetic complications of joint parenthood, but my image."

"But she won't have your memories . . . of anything . . . of us."

"How do you think I will spend my days while you're away? I'll keep them alive, pass them on to my daughter. *My* daughter. It's a pity that it won't be *our* daughter. But next time around you can make even that come true."

She turned her face away from him suddenly, hiding it in the cool leaf shadows of the terrace. But when, after long moments, she turned back to him she was managing to smile.

"And who knows? . . . the records are scanty on this yet . . . that memory might not be transmitted directly through this kind of direct reproduction? That not just my image, but part of *me* may be waiting for you, too? So let's have enough talk of sacrifices. And there are memories still to make. We haven't even started our drinks. Look, the ice has nearly all melted."

She lifted her glass and waited, her face quite serene now, until he lifted his.

THE CLOUDBUILDERS

by

Colin Kapp

In a complete change of style from his "Ethical Engineers" stories in No. 3 ("The Subways of Tazoo") and No. 8 ("The Pen and the Dark"), Colin Kapp writes about a future technology on Earth which has apparently retrogressed to the gas balloon era—but there are some very big differences . . .

THE CLOUDBUILDERS

ONE

CLOSER to the ground now, the field sounds and the forest sounds came up to him with the incredible clarity which never ceased to amaze even though he was no stranger to the air. With only the lightest of breezes, nothing disturbed the fidelity of birdsong and animal cry which reached up as he drifted overhead.

The area was not rich, but he judged it well-provisioned, and that in itself was fortune in these times. Having crossed the sparse lands of the north, and the slag-pits and black fissures which divided the plains, he could appreciate the green fertility and the sense of life abundant and thriving on the ground beneath him. And on the far horizon the great jagged teeth of mountains, falling to the sea, explained why Timor the Cloudbuilder had found it expedient to set his shipyards in this remote corner of the world. Apart from Timor's cloudships, there was no way in or out of this land. No way at all, unless one was brave enough or sufficiently foolish to risk the hazards of the sea.

Jacobi found the prospect rather pleasant. The sun was set high, yet not too hot for the meagre awning of the decking. The air was crisp and fresh, with a heady, crystal clarity, which was balm to eyes and lungs alike. Beyond his reasonable expectation, the slight breezes drifted him as surely towards his destination as if he had set their course himself. This was a day for birds and gods and those who rode the ships the Cloudbuilders made.

There was bread and salt meat in his bag. In the sac was wine, sweet from last year's harvest and tangy with the living fruit. He prepared himself a meal. Above him, the single burner scarcely purred, its blue uniformity of flame no longer visible in the strong sunlight. On the treetops below, the shadow of the great air balloon flitted like Aphrodite's fingertip, lovingly, with an intangible caress. Jacobi had the feeling that he was going to like Catenor.

Although his height was falling slowly, he made no attempt to adjust the burner. For one thing there was little enough gas in the spheres after the last, long leg of his journey and he had a Cloudsman's natural sense of conservation. Secondly, the increasing incidence of farmland over forest suggested he was nearing his destination. By his reckoning, his present course should take him near enough to the shipyards to be seen by the lookout. He searched the scene carefully for the signal smoke which would indicate he had been sighted and give him guidance as to the most opportune time to land. But the fair winds which had carried him from Annonay had placed him near his destination days before he could have been reasonably expected and no lookout would be posted yet unless there were local ships due to return.

It was thus that he saw the clustered town of Catenor two miles to his right, and had already extinguished his burner, before the smoke columns rose to greet him. Choosing a likely field well clear of trees, Jacobi began to manipulate his descent. Gently he grasped the ropes which controlled the great leathern valves at the top of the balloon, venting some of the heated air which carried him, yet carefully retaining sufficient buoyancy to lighten the impact of landing.

With near-perfect conditions and the favour of the gods, his touchdown was as light as a butterfly. As the ground took the weight of the decking, and the rigging began to slacken, he opened the valves to their fullest extent. The breeze carried the deflating balloon lazily sideways clear of the deck as it collapsed and emptied. The fabric was neatly folded and stowed by the time the carts came out to fetch him.

"Welcome to Catenor!" The yardsman from the leading cart held out a work-gnarled hand. "We didn't expect you quite so soon."

"The gods were kind," said Jacobi. "I'd allowed myself three more days at least from Annonay."

The second cart drew up and the work of loading the balloon fabric, decking and ancillary equipment on to the flat drays was begun.

"And how is Lyons these days?" asked the yardsman.

"Prosperous but turbulent. But then, it always was. Do you know Lyons, then?"

"I was apprenticed there before I came to Catenor."

"Ah! That explains why your crew manhandle a ship Guild-fashion. Don't you miss being there?"

"No." The yardsman ran his fingers through the short stubble of his hair. "Lyons was not bad, but it doesn't have the promise of Catenor. The only sore in our sides here is the raiding."

"Raiding?"

"Cloud-pirates from beyond the mountains somewhere. They attack the villages once or twice a year, after beasts or grain or anything else they fancy. The last several times they've even come into Catenor and the yards. We've our own militia now, but they can't be everywhere at once. By the time we get a resistance force to the scene of an attack the chances are the raiders have taken what they wanted and gone back to the clouds again."

"Bad," said Jacobi. "What sort of ships are they using?"

"A mixed collection. Craft they've captured from all

over Europe. Some good, some bad, but there's a rumour they've now got some with engines."

"Engines?" Jacobi was interested. "I've heard of them. There's a Cloudmaster in the Urals who fits engines in his craft. But their great weight destroys most of the advantages."

By this time the loading was complete. Jacobi swung on to the first cart as the patient dray-horses were urged back into life. His eyes alighted on several broad smoke columns rising from the fields about Catenor. He looked at his companion questioningly.

The yardsman was amused. "Oh, that? They're lighting the fires to roast oxen for the feast. Tonight you'll be the guest of honour in the town. It should be a feast worth remembering."

"I'm flattered," said Jacobi. "Do you always greet Journeymen like this?"

His companion laughed. "Not often. But first I have to deliver you to Timor. If you want a tip, don't bow down to him. He respects men who know their own minds and their own worth. He has neither time nor pity for fools. He's a hard man, but you'll find him the best Cloudmaster bar none."

"So I've heard."

"And with your help we'll one day build finer cloudships in Catenor than anything that Annonay can offer."

Timor's face was made of leather, which crinkled to expose a will of iron beneath. He took Jacobi's papers and inspected the seals closely before adding his own. The deeds accepted, Jacobi offered his dagger, as Guild-rule demanded. Timor's weatherbeaten face was crossed suddenly with disbelief. He reached for the instrument, then shook his head.

"Keep it on you, Journeyman. When the raiders come again you may have need of it."

"Cloudmaster, you know I can't do that." Jacobi was firm. "Guild-rule requires I surrender my weapons to you. In law I am your servant and you my protector until my bond here is served. That is our contract and both you and the Guild have sealed it."

"Very well!" Timor's eyes narrowed. "But not all laws made in Annonay will work in Catenor. If the raiders come and I thrust a weapon in your hands I expect you to use it. Either you accept that now or you'd best take your precious contract back to the Guild."

"Perhaps you should have hired a mercenary and not a journeyman?"

"Zeus!" Timor's face clouded with anger. "You call yourself a Cloudsman and you won't take arms even to protect yourself? What kind of cowards are they breeding in Annonay these days? There's no place for unarmed whelps and mewlings in my yards."

"Then your quarrel is with the Guild elders, not with me," said Jacobi quietly. "And if the raiders come, which is the harder thing to do—face them with drawn arms or with folded arms?"

"But where's the sense of it?"

"A Journeyman's duty is only to his calling. Any man may hire him who can pay the Guild the price. He dare not become partisan. His next bond may be with your enemy."

"Even with a cloud-pirate?"

"With any man who has the price. Guild-rule makes no distinctions between men."

The interlude had taken place within the portal of Timor's residence and therefore free from previous interruption. Its privacy was, however, terminated by a clamour from outside as the welcoming procession reached the door. Jacobi looked Timor straight in the eyes.

"Well, Cloudmaster, do you accept the contract, or do I return to Annonay?"

Outside, someone was calling Jacobi's name. A group of girls in the foreground were making giggled dares between themselves and looking into the doorway. The scene was all set for explosive carnival.

Timor pursed his leathern lips. "You stay, of course. If I let you go back to Annonay I doubt if the Guild will send me another. Nemesis take them! Still, the fault is mine. I insisted on a Journeyman of strong mind and strong arm. Now I find I can't stomach the one and can't use the other." The tanned texture of his face broke into a begrudged smile. "Welcome to Catenor, Jacobi. If you hold as firm to the rest of your contract as you have to this, I think I shall be well pleased."

All Catenor, it seemed, was going to the feast. And from the surrounding areas, wherever the word had spread, the country-dwellers came, by farm-cart, ox-cart, horseback and on foot, eager to join the revels.

It was an ideal night. Clear skies and a balmy warmth set a relaxing mood and the slight winds carried exciting hints of roast ox and wood-smoke into the town. Hanging lamps adorned the porches of the houses, and flaring torches, carried in procession or spread among the throng, lit the streets as bright as day. Wearing their brightest dresses, the girls stood out like radiant peacocks in the weaving light: and overall, Dionysus looked down from the clouds and rubbed his hands and smiled and nodded his approval.

Bred in more sophisticated climes, Jacobi was taken aback by the pagan enthusiasm of the gathering. There was a sense of shared relief from fears and deprivations of the past and this Jacobi found difficult to understand. Then suddenly the tide of emotions blossomed forth in a spontaneous flood of greeting and hilarious celebration which was way and above anything the situation seemed to warrant.

He was carried shoulder-high throughout the town and then out to the fields, where the ox-fires cast the cherry glow which made men resemble gods, and women, nymphs. Ale and wine flowed plentifully and the feast was an hilarious, barbaric, greedy parody of a meal. Afterwards, back to the ale waggons and the wine casks and from thence again into the dancing town where everyone knew his name and treated him as a friend.

Although his impressions of the evening were of a continuing whirl of places, scenes and countless people, Jacobi gradually began to discern some faces which he saw more regularly than others. One of these belonged to a remarkably attractive dark-haired girl whose unrestrained vivacity had enlivened the feasting in the field. He remembered drinking wine with her later and a further meeting apparently by chance as he had re-entered the town.

Now she stood close to him, almost inviting his attention. Jacobi did not believe in chance, nor in wasted opportunity. Taking advantage of the congenial melee in the street he moved to her, and, drawing her into a corner, he kissed her. The responses of the girl were as anticipated, but the reaction of the local revellers was one of surprise and near embarrassment. They made him feel as if he had unknowingly performed some act of bravado reckless beyond anticipation even on such a night as this. Since he had been tasting unreluctant lips all evening, he found this disconcerting and inexplicable.

Then somebody cheered and the cheer spread. In a wave of laughter both he and the girl were raised shoulder high and carried triumphantly off through the crowds. Unfortunately the paths of their respective parties diverged and she was gradually lost to his sight. By the time he managed to escape again she was nowhere to be seen.

145

He did not bother to search too long. In the morning there would be time enough to make enquiries, but this was the time for enjoyment. He found another festive group and joined them gleefully, soon losing himself in the wine and the laughter and the sportive company. Finally he trekked with them back to the fields for further meat and song before settling near the warmth of one of the great fires, weary and immeasurably content. It had indeed been a feast worth remembering.

He had scarcely made himself comfortable and was sleepily pondering the crowded events of the day, when somebody splashed wine on his head. Irately he turned, to see the dark-haired girl darting away into the entwined shadows of the couples grouped around the dimming fire. He was now in no mood for a chase, and, having found him, he felt certain she would return. He lay back, but waited like a cat with muscles poised to spring. Another splash of wine and he whirled round with the speed of a tiger and caught at her wrist and held her. Laughingly she dropped the wine-cup and tried to tear herself away, then acquiesced.

"Tell me," Jacobi said, "do you always treat Journeymen this way in Catenor?"

"Not very often." Her eyes, reflecting firelight, were brimful of impudence and mischief. "But then this is rather a special day."

"What makes this day so different from the others?"

"Your coming," she said simply. Something in her manner made him feel that this was no mere coquettish compliment. He pulled her down, then rolled over to the side.

"What's your name?"

"Melanie." She nestled up against him.

"Very well, Melanie. Now tell me why my coming makes this such a special day."

"Why?" She sat up, puzzled. "Because we've waited for

you such a long time, that's why. For years Timor's wanted a Guild Journeyman to teach him how to build the new ships. The Guild offered him a hundred, but he preferred to wait for only Jacobi."

"He'd heard of me before?"

"Heard of you? Jacobi, what are you saying? Three years he's waited to buy your bond for the shipyards. In those three years the raiders have come here seven times. Thirty men are dead in the fighting and more women than I dare to count have been carried to their ships. That's the price we paid for waiting for Jacobi."

"I see." Jacobi did not see at all, but his experience led him to caution. When raiders attacked an otherwise static and feudal society, not all the men died at the raiders' hands and not all the women were carried unwillingly to the marauding cloudships. But his reputation in Catenor seemed unjustified. Other Journeymen had become legends by virtue of their knowledge or their skill or partisan approach. But his own dedication was to science. No one had a right to set him up as demi-god.

"And you think that my coming here is going to change all that?" he asked at last.

She laughed. "Jacobi!"

"Yes?"

"You disappoint me. Are you going to talk all night?"

He pulled her closer. "Sorry! I've much to think about."

He turned his mind to more certain aspects of his reputation. And by the morning she was far from disappointed.

Two

CATENOR was a clean and pleasant town, like most shipyard towns where methane gas was used to fuel the cloudcraft. This was largely because the system of gas production placed a premium on decomposable organic waste.

147

The shipyards were a mile from the town and the road between the town and the yards held plentiful evidence of the enormous underground chambers into which was run the dross and all the field and farmyard waste and the spoilt ends of the harvest. From these chambers Timor extracted his gas for use or sale, and, in return for services received, he distributed the rich manures which kept the soil fertile for so many miles around.

Near the shipyards a small but rapid river turned the waterscrews which powered Timor's reeking line-pumps. In the engine-shed proper the rattle and wheeze of the machinery treating and compressing the gas spoke of large and powerful atmospheric engines, but these were not visible from the road. The treated gas was forced into the strong but lightweight spheres which powered the burners of the cloudcraft. In recent pirate attacks the stock of spheres had been a prime target for the raiders, who both coveted the rich gas and were loath to leave behind undamaged any that they could not take. For this reason Timor kept his stocks of processed gas as low as practical and well protected behind a heavy stockade.

All of these things Jacobi noted as he walked that first morning from the town to the shipyards. With a knowledgeable eye he analysed each stage of Timor's establishment as he came upon it. Timor the Cloudmaster was one of the old tradition of Cloudsmen. With an approach almost wholly empirical he nevertheless constructed in his yards cloudcraft whose durability and range was the envy of many who were better technically endowed. Only the strong influence of the Guild had succeeded in producing craft superior to Timor's and now Timor was trying to even the balance by importing Guild knowledge and science to back his own skill and expertise. But it was an importation which promised to be more fruitful than ever Timor hoped.

Jacobi knew that by the end of his bond in Catenor the wheeze of the atmospheric engines would be replaced by the sharper hiss and rattle of high pressure steam reciprocating engines, and the steam-turbine would not be far away from discovery. At a guess, the waterscrews would also disappear, as new efficiencies in the gas compressors outstripped the capacity of the old line pumps to move sufficient gas from the tanks. Perhaps, with the shaft-power and the techniques and ideas he would leave behind him, some in Catenor would even begin to experiment with the unfamiliar concepts of a strange force called electricity. And these things would be incidental to his contribution to the methods of building cloudcraft.

It was less than an hour after dawn and a crisp chill still inhabited the air, but the yards were already alive with activity. Axemen were shaping spars and deck timbers with the sharp snick of steel on firm wood. Blacksmiths' forges glowed with the regular pulse of the bellows, and hammer and anvil chimed a chorus which had everything but melody. In the spinning shed the song of women denoted the satisfactory progress of making ropes and rigging. Only the fabric shed held its accustomed silence as sharp-eyed seamstresses sewed the myriad tiny stitches to form the seams in the fabric panels from which the great balloons were made.

Timor was in his office. Jacobi knocked and entered, a trifle hesitant after his first encounter with the Cloudmaster. True to his reputation, Timor wasted no time in coming to the point.

"Is it true, Jacobi, that in Annonay the Guild yards are building cloudships which have no need for burners?"

Jacobi nodded. "True enough. They are filled with a gas called hydrogen, which is lighter than the air itself. They have no need for heat."

"Lighter than air?" Timor seemed about to dispute the statement. Then he stopped and spread his hands. "If you

149

say it, then it must be so. Tell me, do these ships stay buoyant permanently without the need for fuel?"

"They lose a little gas, which has to be replaced. But substantially it's so."

"I see!" Timor considered for a moment. "Then a ship that needs no fuel for buoyancy has an almost unlimited range, and the cost of flight is low?"

"Yes."

"But if they have all these advantages, why do we not see more of them?"

"One day we shall, when we know better how to build and handle them. At the moment they're dangerous and tiresome craft to fly. Because of their inbuilt buoyancy there is no easy control of ascent and descent as on a normal cloudcraft. They are not easily landed to wait for wind-change and they are more happily moored to towers than brought to the ground."

"Strange craft," said Timor thoughtfully. "Could we build one here in Catenor?"

"If you have coal, furnace builders and boilermakers, yes. You have already everything else that is needed."

"And you will show us how?"

"My knowledge is yours, Timor. But don't underestimate either the difficulties or the dangers of the venture."

"Difficulties and dangers are part of the stock in trade of a Cloudsman," said Timor. "But I'll bear it in mind. Build me a hydrogen ship such as they build in Annonay. When it comes to flying it, I have some of the finest Cloudsmen alive. With their skill and your knowledge, we'll learn to tame it. If such ships can do what you describe, then craft from Catenor will one day circle the world."

Jacobi smiled slightly. "A noble ambition, Cloudmaster."

"Aye! But not an impossible one. By all accounts the ancients used to do it."

"So the legends have it."

"Legends?" Timor's eyes were direct and challenging. "I had heard that in Annonay the achievements of the ancients were more than legend."

Jacobi shrugged. "Of gods and ancients there are always many tales. For myself, I find it better use of time to study the craft of cloudships."

"Indeed?" Timor was critical. "Your reputation says otherwise. They credit you with much knowledge of the ancients' science. I suggest that cloudships are merely an exercise in application."

Jacobi faced Timor squarely. "An intriguing speculation, Cloudmaster."

"But a true one, eh? No, don't worry. All that passes within these walls is between us two alone. But if we're to work together it's better that we understand each other fully."

"I think we already understand each other, Cloudmaster. But I'd be interested to know what gave you the notion."

"Deduction. Journeymen from the Guild come always to teach—never to learn. So who teaches the Guild? Where does all the knowledge come from?"

"That you must ask the Guild elders."

"I already have, but they were even more devious than you. Nemesis take them! So I draw my own conclusions. I suspect they have some oracle, some means of access to the knowledge of the ancients."

"Even if it were true," said Jacobi, "what difference would it make?"

Timor spread his hands expressively. "Knowledge is power, Jacobi. And with that sort of knowledge available to them, the Guild ought to be the most powerful force in the world."

"But it isn't," said Jacobi mildly.

"It doesn't appear to be. And there's the mystery of it.

The Guild is influential, yes, but they seem to do no more than instruct in the building of cloudcraft."

"Doesn't that rather tend to disprove your theory, then?"

"No." The Cloudmaster's shrewd eyes searched Jacobi's face carefully. "No, it rather tells me they have some very good reason for acting as they do. I should dearly love to know what that reason is. In fact, I intend to find out somehow. So let me warn you, Jacobi, if you want to keep your secret, maintain your guard carefully. Because there's more than I hold to this theory and some who would go to even greater lengths than I to find the answer."

The big trunk which was the centrepiece of his possessions had a covering of tough, tanned hide, deep-shone from years of burnishing and wax, patterned with brass studs and fitted with a massive hinge. The lock, a rare example of the artistry and skill of some craftsman worker in brass, was disfigured only where a thief had once used a crowbar in an abortive attempt to force it open. But Jacobi was unworried by the threat of attempted theft. Under the hide and the brass and the hints of underlying oak which showed at scuffed corners, was a casket of forged vanadium steel and the wards and tumblers which guarded the lock were products of another age and not likely to yield to any tools or crafts available in Catenor.

He had deliberately sought lodgings in the town, away from the shipyards and from the living quarters usually provided. The gods had favoured his search and he had secured a high attic room, comfortably furnished, covering the entire area of the house. The several dormer windows admitted ample light by day and provided good views over the surrounding country. Now, under the rough-hewn beams of the low and sloping ceiling, he had a chance to be alone and unobserved. Jacobi checked the door, then opened the trunk and took out a device which he laid upon the table. He thumbed it into activity and waited impatiently for the go-ahead tell-tale to show.

"Jacobi calling Annonay Control."

There was a moment's hesitation before the device answered.

"Annonay Control answering." The voice was accompanied by a rushing background like the sound of waves on a seashore. "Come in, Jacobi. How's progress?"

"Good," said Jacobi. "As we suspected, Timor has his suspicions about what the Guild is doing, but he's no idea how or why it's being done. Fortunately his curiosity is going to make him very receptive to new ideas. I suggest we push up the pace in Catenor just as fast as they can absorb it."

"Agreed," said the voice of Annonay Control. "Progress has been far too slow in Catenor and the west and too fast in Annonay. The discrepancy's beginning to show. There's even talk of moving the Guild yards out of Annonay to slow things down a bit."

"I guessed it might come to that," Jacobi said. "No matter how well you keep a secret, something always leaks. Catenor would be a good place for a new Guild yard if I can cut down the raiding."

"Is it that serious?"

"Not so far, but it threatens to become so. Apparently the raiders have got some craft with engines now and if they follow the advantage along the usual lines they could stifle Catenor before I can really get it started."

"I'll look into it. I doubt if the elders will sanction direct action against the raiders, but they'll probably give you discretionary powers to play the situation to the best advantage for Catenor."

"Discretionary powers would be all I'd need," said Jacobi. "I'll be in touch later."

"Right! I'll put this to the elders and see if I can get you a quick decision. And, Jacobi . . ."

"Yes?"

"Promise me something. You've a tough job ahead and we can't afford complications. Leave the women alone."

"Nemesis forbid that I touch one!" said Jacobi.

"That's no damned answer and you know it. I tell you, Jacobi, one day you're going to put a woman before Guild principles. And on that day you're going to make a mistake. But with the type of merchandise we're handling, we just daren't make mistakes. People have set the world on fire for much, much less."

Jacobi turned off the device, but looked at it thoughtfully for a long while before putting it away. Its compact heaviness stemmed largely from the crystal and ceramic blocks within: solid-state fully-integrated monolithic circuits and the imperishable Seebeck-effect fissile semiconductor generator—techniques from the age of miracles. Yet to him the device was neither an anachronism nor was it futuristic. It was simply one of those accepted portions of his life which, except in Guild circles, must forever remain in the shadows. And Jacobi was aware that the shadows folded more closely round him every day.

Finally he closed the trunk and locked it and lit the dim oil lamp, for the night was closing in. Somebody had left him roses in a vase on the table, and the scent, unnoticed until this moment, made him think of lips and wine and a girl called Melanie . . . Melanie with the night-dark hair and a way of making love which was scorching like the sun. Slowly the shadows grew in the dormer alcoves and extended from the huge, untidy beams until the symbolism of the room became an exacting analogue of his life and his projected future. And at that point Jacobi reacted to his unreasoning compulsion—and left the room in search of life and light.

There was a tavern off the main street where the sounds of cheerful expression exceeded the capacity of the brewhouse to keep it confined. The light and the laughter and the music spilled from the doors and windows in a friendly tide which spread across the gutter and irresistibly attracted his feet. Entering, he chanced upon the yardsman who had met him on his arrival in Catenor. The fellow greeted him heartily, ordered ale, then drew Jacobi aside conspiratorially.

"You're a rare lad, Jacobi. You know, you'd quite a reputation even before you arrived. But you've a better'n now—or a worse'n, depending on how you look at it." He nudged Jacobi in the ribs with his elbow.

"You're way ahead of me," said Jacobi guardedly. "I'd been drinking much. What did I do?"

"Do?" The yardsman nudged him again. "There's not many men in Catenor who'd dare lay Timor's daughter— even if she'd give them the chance, which she wouldn't."

"Timor's daughter? You mean the girl Melanie is Timor's daughter?"

"Zeus! Do you mean you didn't know it? I'll wager Timor's not been able to find you today, else you'd not be left in doubt."

"I spent most of the day with him," said Jacobi. "But he never said a word of it. Perhaps he doesn't know."

The yardsman's brow clouded. "Nothing happens in Catenor that Timor doesn't know. Take a tip from me, lad. Tread very warily. Timor and his daughter were both stamped from the same clay. They neither of them give anything except that they expect back a great deal more for it. Just ask yourself, Jacobi, what is it they're expecting to get from you." The yardsman turned back to his friends. "Here, lads, what do you make of this . . ."

Jacobi joined them in the drinking and the friendly badinage, while some more serious part of his mind attempted to analyse the situation. He ignored his previous feelings of pride because he realised now that the conquest had been too easy. Last night she had been the hunter and he the hunted—and Timor had held his peace about it. Or had he? Jacobi held the memory of the shrewd eyes on his face and the voice which said: "... and some who would go to even greater lengths than I to find the answer."

But just how much did Timor expect to get in return for his daughter?

THREE

TIMOR fetched a master black-iron boilermaker from his workplace near the forests. The furnace makers came a hundred miles by cloudcraft on the first good winds, listened to Jacobi's proposal, and shook their heads. Then they decided to stay. Jacobi, fighting the lack of established technology which a Guild yard would have given him, was patient. He modified and simplified his designs to suit the tools and skills available, hoping that he could achieve his aim without sacrificing safety. He alone was conscious of the more subtle aspects of the exercise. Given the need for a product and the certainty that it could be made, the techniques for its production would grow like seeds in men's minds. If he could manage to build one plant for producing hydrogen in Catenor, then others would far more easily be able to build similar plants in the future.

For the quantity and purity of the hydrogen he needed, he decided to build two complementary plants: an iron-steam retort for producing the hydrogen itself, and a water-gas generator to regenerate the sponge-iron bed in the retort. An alternative scheme to produce hydrogen also directly from water-gas he dismissed because of the practical difficulties of building scrubbers to remove the unwanted carbon di- and monoxides.

A small coke-making plant was also necessary and he planned to contain some of the coal-gas by-product both to assist in heating his retorts and also to introduce the inhabitants of Catenor to its uses. Thus an offshoot of his work would be the founding of at least one new basic industry in Catenor which would grow in time without his further intervention.

Absorbed in the problems of planning such an ambitious venture and one which involved him as designer, inventor, overseer and the source of almost all the knowledge it required, Jacobi almost daily worked himself to a standstill. He frequently slept on the site amid the tools and drawings, being too tired even to journey to his room in Catenor. Under these conditions he almost forgot the dark-haired Melanie, having neither the time nor the energy for pursuit or conquest. After many days of such activity, Timor, fearing for Jacobi's health, ordered him to rest. Jacobi went to his room at midday and slept the twenty-four hours round.

He awoke to the scent of roses from the fresh blooms on the table and leaped rapidly out of bed, realising that someone had visited him while he slept. He found no sign of the intruder, however, except that yesterday's dead rose petals had been swept into the basket. Checking the door, he turned to the trunk and set the communication device on the table. As he pressed the switch the print-out slot at the bottom began to issue a white card. He picked it up and read its legend.

> —ANNONAY CONTROL TO JACOBI—URGENT—GUILD APPROVES YOU FULL DISCRETIONARY POWERS AGAINST RAIDERS—IMPERATIVE UPGRADING OF CATENOR PROCEEDS AS PLANNED—ANNONAY SITUATION IMBALANCE BECOMING CRITICAL—END—

Jacobi was about to make verbal contact with Annonay,

then thought better of it. Even in the daylight, another wrap of shadows seemed to close around his shoulders and he was suddenly depressed at the sheer weight of the obligations which were pressing on his head. Some beast inside him clawed out to establish a personal freedom which he knew he might never attain. Guild merchandise was indeed a dangerous and heavy weight to carry.

A footstep on the stair leading to his attic broke his reverie. He locked the device securely in the trunk before he dared open the door. It was Melanie, with kisses, fresh pies, bread and wine. Jacobi, having just awakened from sleep, had not realised how great was his appetite. And later, as the setting sun red-bloomed the ceiling with its light, they both sat down to eat.

It was only afterwards, when Melanie had gone, that Jacobi looked for the white card bearing the message from Annonay—and found that it was missing. In this he sensed he had already made a mistake of the kind about which Annonay had warned. But even so, he reckoned that he had gained the best of the bargain from the unintended contract. He knew now that Timor's curiosity must be as insatiable as was his daughter's passion for love. And these were both factors he could use to the Guild's or his own advantage.

Having ensured that the construction of the hydrogen plant was well started, Jacobi turned his attention to the making of the hydrogen ship itself. This was not so difficult, since most of the techniques were common with those Timor already used. But the work involved a lot of calculations which were foreign to Timor's empirical approach. In design detail, too, there were alterations to be made. Jacobi insisted that the iron links and bolt eyes normally employed round the deck-yoke were replaced by fixtures of wrought brass, to eliminate the possible danger from sparks. He wanted a mooring tower, too, but he originally dismissed the idea because, without engines available, he knew that once the craft had left the tower no wind, however favourable, could ever drift it back to that precise point for mooring. But Timor over-ruled the objection, and ordered the tallest firs to be cut from the forest and trimmed and erected to make a scaffold of sufficient height to launch the ship.

The coke-making plant was the first thing in operation. Timor was more interested in the tar than in the coal-gas itself, but Jacobi made lime-light burners which were far brighter than the torches used round the yards, and the yardsmen were quick to adopt them. Meanwhile his stocks of coke grew to a useful volume.

It was during this period that the raiders made their next appearance. Jacobi was in the yards with Timor, explaining details of how hydrogen could be safely conveyed from the retort to the ship. Above them a dark and sultry sky showed the imminence of rain. The yards were already apprehensive. This was the raiding season and a low cloud-belt with suitable winds formed the most advantageous conditions and cover for the cloud raiders. Lookouts had already been posted on the towers and no one was surprised to hear the horns and the cries of : "Raiders ho!"

Typical of their pattern of attack, the raiders had travelled far and were now returning on home winds. Thus they could descend at will, secure their prize, and escape to the clouds again safe in the knowledge that any who dared to follow must drift into the dangerous mountain region which was raider's territory. Had they attempted a raid while borne on outward winds, Timor's crews would have taken to the air and followed them into some final battle precipitated by the lesser range of the marauding cloud-craft. But no craft from Timor's yards had ever returned once having entered the mountains.

The lookouts were eagle-sharp in their perception and both Timor and Jacobi had to scan the sky to locate the points already identified as raiding craft. Timor saw them first and uttered an oath of annoyance.

"The carrion!" he said. "Only three, but this time they've got engines. Where's our defence against that?"

The question was rhetorical and Jacobi made no answer. His searching eyes found the objects and even at that range he could see that Timor was right. At the rear of each deck squatted a black bulk of mechanism with a shaft trailing crude wings which flailed huge circles in the air. The effect of the wings was slight, but for combat the ability to move even slightly faster than the wind, or to resist it, gave its possessor a crucial advantage. Timor's craft, like all normal cloudships, had control of ascent and descent, but for speed and direction they were utterly dependent on the winds.

The raiders, however, had a further advantage. Besides conferring a degree of control over the speed, the engines also gave a limited manoeuvrability. This was being demonstrated now. Their ships were not following the wind but moving cross-wind at a slow angle so as to bring their course more nearly over the shipyards. To achieve this they were using canvas keels on a framework set aslant under the decking, which, combined with the thrust from the rotating wings, angled their ships untidily crabwise but gave them some choice of direction.

Jacobi could sense Timor's mixed anger and interest as the unorthodox craft drifted nearer to his yards. This was certainly not a raiding party. With only three ships, each carrying but a handful of men, they would have fared badly had they attempted to land. More probably it was a scouting expedition assessing the potentialities of the harvest in preparation for a future raid. Given fair winds they would come again one day soon with a hundred ships or more, armed and able to take whatever they needed or fancied.

"Jacobi." The Cloudmaster had moved to his side, still gazing at the ships in the sky. "If I could get one of those engines, could you make it work for me?"

"Yes. Or copy it and build more. But they're too heavy for your kind of voyaging. You need too much gas for the burners in order to maintain buoyancy. That limits your range."

"But your hydrogen ship could carry one without limiting its range."

"True!"

"Good!" Timor had come to a sudden decision. He dashed across the yards yelling orders to his crews. At first Jacobi failed to understand his intention, but suddenly the import of the conversation struck home to him.

At four points in the yards tethered craft, with balloons filled and ground-based auxiliary burners idling, had been prepared for flight and were waiting for a wind-change that would drift them south-east with cargoes of pigs for sale. The squeal of swine being hastily released into the yards and the running flurry of men, told of a rapidly conceived change of purpose. Shipborne burners flared high and luminous as scratch crews hastened to prepare the ships for flight. As the craft were readied Timor bade them stay as he watched the speed and direction of the raiders' ships above, anxious not to rise too soon and be carried by the wind helplessly out of the field of battle.

Jacobi moved too, as soon as he realised what Timor meant to do. The dark cloud-cover and the impending rain gave him a sudden inspiration. He ran to the workshop wherein he kept his tools and personal belongings. In his satchel was a waterproof pouch, tight-folded and bound to form a seal. He hooked the pouch to his belt and took out also a short rodlike weapon with a grip to fit his hand. Then he ran back to where Timor's cloudcraft still strained at their moorings. Noting the position of the raiders, he chose the ship he judged most likely to make a near interception and climbed aboard, swinging up the rigging like a monkey.

Timor was on the decking and saw him pass. He raised a quizzical eyebrow and seemed to shout something, but no words came to Jacobi's ears. Jacobi reached the fabric of the balloon and continued on up the rigging net outside the huge envelope, his toes digging into the soft fabric belly. Then, at Timor's signal, the mooring ropes were axed, and the four cloudships rose from the yards in slow unison in an attempt to intercept and come to grips with the raiders.

It was a good attempt, but one doomed to failure from the start. The air in Timor's balloons had grown over-hot in the period of waiting and the craft rose at a faster than usual rate. Though the burners were quickly doused, Timor's ships achieved the altitude of the raiders too soon, and continued rising. Some of Timor's men had crossbows, but the punctures made by steel shafts in the fabric of the raiders' balloons were too small to do material damage. Likewise they were too high and too distant to accurately find targets on the raiders' decks. Their only chance was to try and close the separation to a point where they could ensnare the raiders' rigging with barbed grapples and haul the vessels together.

Frantically Timor's ships vented air in an attempt to fall closer to the raiders' level. But the process was slow and the enemy craft had abruptly changed course. Since he could control only the height and not the position of his craft, the situation was out of Timor's hands. The raiders' new direction was calculated to take them out of grapple and bow-shot range in the shortest possible time, and, incidentally, proved the superiority of engines in combat or defence.

Almost atop the balloon now, with his feet wedged securely between the fabric and the rigging, Jacobi waited, watching the raiders' ships behind and below wheel to the new course which Timor would be unable to follow. Then his heart leaped as he saw the implications of the move. Given luck, the right-hand ship of the three, moving slowly sideways and at a speed slightly greater than that of the wind, would soon pass reasonably close below the craft on which he sat. He opened his waterproof pouch with particular care, then took up the weapon with the hand-grip and bent it savagely.

The mechanism clicked satisfactorily and he straightened it and opened the breech. In the pouch were darts with long, thin, metal splines and a curious head. He fitted one into the weapon and sighted it on the raiders' balloon, waiting his opportunity. A few rainspots thudding on the fabric around him reminded him to close the pouch securely. For some minutes it seemed as if his plan might come to nothing. The target craft on which his attention was centred was drawing rapidly off of their course and the venting of the balloon on which he rode was reducing the height difference without bringing them closer together.

He finally judged the approach of the two ships to be about the nearest that they would achieve, though the range was still too far for certainty. Raising his weapon he took careful aim at the target balloon. The weapon responded with the phut of released air, but there was no way of knowing if his dart had found a target or fallen into empty air. Swiftly he reloaded and re-primed his weapon and sent his darts winging one by one. Above them the rainclouds hovered dark and the forests below were still and saddened by shades of black. Now only time would tell if his missiles had found their intended place of lodging.

He became aware slowly that he was not alone. Timor had climbed the rigging on the other side and had been watching his activities with interest. He moved round and took Jacobi's weapon and examined it curiously.

163

"If crossbows can't get me an engine, what chance d'you think you have with this? Or was it crows you were after?" The last sentence was less of a question than a probe for further information.

Jacobi maintained a bland face. "Gaining an engine is your affair, Timor. Never let it be said that a Cloudmaster looks for the help of a whelp or mewling. And even the crows were cleverer than I."

Timor scanned him narrowly. Although they were by this time at roughly the same level as the raiders' balloons, the divergent paths of the two forces had placed their distance apart too far now even for bowshot. But Jacobi continued to follow the progress of his quarry closely.

"You're up to some mischief," said Timor. "Else you'd not have come."

"I?" Innocently.

"Yes, Jacobi. There's far more to your scheming than the building of cloudcraft."

"Do you have any complaints about the way I serve my bond?"

"Quite the contrary. You've achieved more progress in a few weeks than most men accomplish in a lifetime. That's what makes me suspicious. It doesn't escape me that everything you do has at least two purposes."

"Nemesis take the thought! How badly do you want that engine?"

"If I cannot match the raiders in the sky then I had better stop shipbuilding in Catenor."

"That's what I thought," said Jacobi. "When the raiders are far enough crosswind they'll stop using their engines—they take too much fuel to use for other than short manoeuvres. After that they'll drift with the winds and rely on us not following them into the mountains. Maintain your height and stay with them. It could just be that one of them won't get that far."

"I see!" Timor's eyes were like bright steel coins in wrinkled pigskin purses. "They didn't tell me that prognostication was also one of your talents."

"I'm no adept. I could do with a little assistance."

"In what way?"

"Pray for rain," said Jacobi.

Four

As Jacobi had predicted, the raiding ships, having drawn far enough crosswind to be free from molestation, stopped their engines and drifted with the same winds that carried Timor's ships. Thus there was a period of enforced stalemate during which the pirate ships strove to gain height, and Timor's ships to follow them.

Jacobi maintained his station atop the balloon, watching the growing rainclouds and the darkening ridges of the mountains towards which they were being carried. Under the mountains the broad estuary of the river showed like a band of steel dividing the fertile lands from the grey rock slopes.

Time was becoming important. If the rain came before the drifting forces reached the river, they would most probably gain their prize. But if it held off for longer, then the raiders would drift home to the sanctuary of the mountains and Timor would not dare to follow them across the water. If Timor's ships crossed to the mountains they would isolate themselves from help or return on the ground and would have to set-down in the mountain reaches to await a wind-change. This might well involve a long encampment, and, due to the haste of their departure, the party had come recklessly unprovisioned. Further, falling into raiders' territory, they could expect no help or mercy from pirates anxious to add new cloudcraft to their stolen fleet.

But a closer misfortune was at hand for Timor's ship. In the yards the cloudcraft had been readied waiting for wind-change using ground-based auxiliary burners to conserve the gas charge in the flight spheres. The latter had been standing near the craft and had been hastily coupled when the emergency ascent began. Unfortunately something had been overlooked. The sphere of gas powering the burner on which their buoyancy depended, broke suddenly from its straps and plummeted downward. The loss of its weight shot the ship rapidly skyward before it began its slow, inevitable fall as the air in the balloon grew cooler.

Jacobi felt the ship lift as the sphere fell away and the cries of dismay from below explained the nature of the mishap. He could have wept with frustration, for the growing patter of raindrops indicated that, the gods willing, a few minutes longer might have placed the raiders' ship and its engine at their mercy. Nor was he deceived as to the seriousness of the situation facing Timor's vessel.

He felt the rigging under him slacken and his weight begin to sink into the fabric as the warm air inside the balloon grew less supporting. The men from the deck below were climbing now to join him, the safest place aboard a crashing cloudship being above the fabric, with something beneath to cushion the impact of landing and less chance of being smothered by the collapsing envelope. But at this height their chance of survival was less than even and fear inhabited their eyes.

Their companion ships, seeing their plight, began to fall also—initially faster since they could afford to vent hot air, while Timor could not. Timor's concern was to retain every vestige of buoyancy which the cooling air in the balloon could give them, but they were still dangerously high and he had no real hope of succeeding. Jacobi stayed aloft a moment longer, watching the craft in which he was sure his darts were buried and praying for effect from the now freely falling rain.

The gods were suddenly pleased. From the balloon and rigging of the raiders' ship patches of fire sprang up, clearly visible even from the growing distance. The fires were quickly extinguished, but were sufficiently damaging to make holes in the fabric through which a man might have put his head. Then the crippled raider too began to fall.

The plight of Timor's craft was now perilous indeed. The angle of their descent threatened to drift them across the water to strike the mountain's foot with killing force and Timor dared not sharpen the angle by venting air, since this could only have increased their speed of impact. Summing up the situation rapidly, Jacobi clambered untidily down the slackening rigging and found Timor alone on the deck- ing.

Timor forced a wry smile at his appearance. "What now, Journeyman. Does the Guild have answers for this situation too?"

"Yes," said Jacobi. "Get those men down and do as I do. It's our only chance."

Climbing back up the rigging to the point where the ropes just cleared the bottom of the envelope, he reached through the lines with a blade and slashed at the fabric. Timor watched him for one second before divining his purpose, then moved like a fury, cursing and slashing with his knife, and calling to the rest of the crew to do likewise. As the great circle was cut from the bottom of the balloon, the burner and its harness fell away. Shorn of this weight and open to the air, the half-balloon flowered outward like a giant mushroom within the confines of the rigging, its speed of descent checking perceptibly.

Then Jacobi directed their attention downwards and they cut the main ropes holding, at the lowest possible points.

The decking fell dramatically away, leaving the men suspended in the rigging with the giant fabric mushroom now wildly unstable and threatening to spill air and collapse. But with the help of the gods and under the lashing of Timor's blasphemous tongue they managed to re-locate their weight and maintain the stability of their precious canopy. Again their speed was checked, but even then several of them would have come to harm had they not fallen into the waters of the estuary.

As his head broke the surface of the water, Jacobi struggled and freed himself from the ropes and rigging and struck out for the nearest land. He was a poor swimmer and he seriously doubted his ability to swim the distance. Certainly he had no capacity to go back and ensure that the others were free and able to escape. He swam doggedly towards a clump of trees which was all he could see of the shore, hoping that the cramp, which so frequently terminated his swimming would not strike before he could reach safety.

For a long while his efforts seemed unable to decrease his distance from the trees and he began to lose hope. He was tiring rapidly with the unaccustomed exercise and his swimming had become a mode of spasmodic snatches at the water, wasteful of energy and unhelpful towards progress. Then cramp knotted the muscles in his right leg and in a momentary panic he twisted and sank untidily and painfully in the water.

He came up gasping for breath and spitting water and perilously near to drowning. But strong hands seized his shoulders and he allowed himself to float and be drawn by the arm towards the shore. Then he was commanded to put down his feet and he found himself standing with the water waist high on the soft sands. His rescuer supported him on his arm until Jacobi had managed to overcome the cramp in his legs sufficiently to limp his way to dry land.

Exhausted, Jacobi sank on to the bank for a while, then looked about. As far as he could gather, all the members of the ship's crew were now safely ashore. He noticed Timor farther along the bank, face down on his arms and covered in mud from the low basin through which he had crawled from the water. Even from a distance he could see Timor's shoulders moving convulsively, and, fearing that the Cloudmaster was ill, Jacobi ran to him and turned him over. But it was laughter that racked Timor's frame. Seeing Jacobi, he stopped and sat up and clapped a huge and muddy arm around the Journeyman's shoulder.

"By the gods, Jacobi, for a non-combatant you do a remarkable line in warfare and survival!"

Jacobi sat down beside him. "Did you think then that all that came from Annonay was academic?"

"No. I expected common sense as well. But not miracles. What did you do to the raiders' ship?"

"I shot darts at them tipped with a metal called sodium. The sodium was coated to protect it in my pouch, but when exposed to moisture the coat dissolved and the metal caught fire."

"Metal caught fire?" Timor looked at him quickly, then shrugged. "Strange tools for a Guild journeyman, to be sure. Do they have a peaceful use as well?"

"No."

"I thought not," said Timor. "I always knew there was more to the Guild than sweetness and light. What now of your claim to be non-partisan?"

"I fired those darts in the Guild's interests, not in yours."

"I see! And how do you in Catenor determine what is in the interests of the Guild?"

"You already know that, Timor—or if you don't, ask Melanie."

"Zeus!" said Timor ruefully. "I should have known better than to bandy words with you." He searched in his soaking clothes for a pocket and from this he produced the wet and crumpled remains of what once had been Jacobi's message card from Annonay. "Nemesis take all double-devious journeymen! I've wronged you, Jacobi lad, and I freely admit it. I was suspicious of you and your overt cleverness. I still am, but I know now it's working in my favour. You build me a new ship, destroy my enemy and save my life. For that I repay you by doubting your motives and stealing your messages."

"And lending me your daughter," said Jacobi mischievously.

Timor's smile broke through again. "You won't be drawn, will you, Jacobi. I respect you for that, though I'm damned if I'll let the matter rest."

Soon they heard the horns through the thicknesses of the forest and answered with loud cries, having no horns of their own with which to answer. Fortunately they were heard and soon located by the crews of Timor's other ships which had made safe landing. A camp had been established and a brushwood fire had been started, the wet wood being kindled with methane from a flight sphere.

The remains of the damaged raiders' ship was found caught in the trees about two miles away. The crew were dead and the deck was torn and splintered, but the precious engine was almost intact and easily recoverable. Timor himself directed its lowering to the ground, with patient care. For him this was the start of a new era in Catenor and he would permit no risk which might endanger his prize. Finally the job was done and the engine, still on torn fragments of decking, was gently laid on the forest loam to await the drays from Catenor to carry it back to the yards.

When Jacobi examined the mechanism he found, not the crude gas engine he had expected, but a fairly advanced diesel, and he then knew for a certainty just how serious the situation in Annonay had become.

With Timor now even more solidly behind him, Jacobi now found himself in almost complete control of the Catenor yards and work on the hydrogen ship project moved ahead at a furious pace. The hydrogen plant was completed and ready for testing long before the ship itself had been constructed. Jacobi's daily round was long, arduous and exacting, but he found time to go to Catenor each evening to relax and see Melanie. After three weeks, and with her father's blessing, she chose to become his mistress and moved in with him in the high attic room. Thus stabilised, Jacobi put his mind and hands solidly to work.

The stormclouds of trouble brewing over Annonay left him largely untouched. Guild merchandise was explosive media and needed to be handled with caution even by those bred in its service. An uncontrolled leak of advanced technology from Annonay into a world not yet prepared to receive it, had given great advantages to an unscrupulous few and public opinion had swung sharply against the Guild. This was a breach of confidence which only time itself could heal. In the meantime the Guild had no option but to reduce the scope of its operations in Annonay to that of building established forms of cloudcraft.

Six weeks later Jacobi's project was complete. The hydrogen plant was fully operational and a competent crew had been instructed in its use. The ship itself, now containing on its deck the diesel engine and a fair reserve of fuel, lay at the foot of the mooring scaffold waiting for the charge of gas which would make it buoyant without burners. The wings which the raiders had used on the engine had gone and in their place a wooden propeller occupied the shaft, while a system of rudders had been provided for direction. Tomorrow was to be the day of the first flight. Jacobi's last checks gave him confidence that the venture would be a success. He returned to Melanie full of confidence.

Against Guild-rule, he had no longer made a secret of his communication device since Melanie had moved in. Now it stood permanently on a small table ready for his nightly contact with Annonay. Melanie left the instrument severely alone, realising, by some instinct, that it was part of another age and had powers and contents whose secrets she would never comprehend. This factor, more than anything, brought home to Jacobi the separation which would always be between them and wrapped the insufferable shades of isolation more firmly round his shoulders.

This day when he arrived home she complained that the instrument had been clicking to itself as if trying to attract attention. Jacobi inspected the message store. The tell-tale indicated that something was contained therein, so he activated the print-out. He was both prepared and yet unprepared for the message he received.

> —TECHNICAL INFORMATION RETRIEVAL CENTRE NEW YORK—VIA SATELLITE LINK AND LA GAUDE SUB-CENTRE—TO JACOBI IN CATENOR—MESSAGE BEGINS QUOTE CRISIS SITUATION—RIOTING IN ANNONAY—GUILD YARDS ABANDONED—EUROPEAN OPERATIONS ENDANGERED—IMPERATIVE YOU SECURE CATENOR FOR NEW GUILD YARD—NEGOTIATE TIMOR ANY BASIS UNQUOTE—END MESSAGE—
>
> —YORKTOWN CONTROL—

Jacobi caught the card in his hand and, after scanning it briefly, he slipped it into his pocket without a word to Melanie. Later he tried to raise Annonay Control on verbal contact, but received nothing but static from a distant storm. As the message had inferred, the Annonay installation was finished. Whether later historians would see this as the end of an era which failed, or merely as a temporary setback to one of the braver ventures of mankind, was now largely in his own hands. But his hands were already tired from continuous overwork and the brain which guided them was likewise tired of too much knowing, too much thinking, too many obligations—and a brand of loneliness which held him apart from Melanie even in the throes of love.

He found suddenly that he needed time to think, to question seriously, perhaps for the first time in his life, whether the purpose for which the Guild existed was an ideal worth what it demanded of him. It would be too easy to slip into the pattern of life at Catenor, to marry Melanie, to raise children, to build cloudcraft in Timor's yards and to forget the Guild and its intrigues and obligations and its dedication to an abstraction called posterity. He remembered acutely the whip of his own anger against those who had inexplicably weakened and deserted. Only now could he see how immature it was to judge until one had oneself been tested and how little you could predict of your own reactions under the duress of emotion and overwork.

Melanie must have intuitively sensed the conflict within him and how crucially she was involved, for she drew him to her and soothed him and when they fell to making love it was tenderly and with a great consideration utterly unlike the passionate consummations of the past. Jacobi drifted into sleep still in her arms, but restlessly, his dreams confused with vaulted banks of microfilm and microfiche and ranks of reading-screens, video playback monitors and electron flying-spot decoders. Again the voice of his mentor led him through the complex concepts of computerised normal text awareness and reconstructed in painstaking detail the elements of computer programming for data retrieval. When he awoke, overhot and unrested, to the sound of horns and cries of: "Raiders ho!", he had some difficulty in determining reality from dreaming.

His confusion was enhanced by the fact that he knew that a pirate raid at such a time was a near impossibility. Firstly, the raiders never came in darkness and secondly the winds had set to outwind as far as the raiders were concerned. It would have taken a very confident raider—or a very mad one—to land in Catenor under such conditions. Or a very powerful group of raiders!

The last thought crystallised as a shattering possibility. Knowing that Timor had both a Journeyman and an engine, the raiders could have realised that opposition from Timor's sector was destined to become increasingly stiffer, ending, as such developments must, in the final destruction of random raiding forces. The logical counter-move in such circumstances was a massed strike with all available man-power to stifle the potential opposition while it was still in embryo. That meant the yards would be the focal point of the attack, and destruction, not plunder, would be the object of the exercise.

Then Jacobi knew that his previous conflict had been resolved. He could see now that the opposite to the Guild's principle was a sort of painful barbarian anarchy—a hang-over of the last dark age out of which they were still trying to claw their way. He dressed hastily, and Melanie, waking after him, sat up in a spasm of panic and clutched at his wrist.

"Jacobi, don't leave me!"

He drew his arm away carefully. "I have to get to the yards, Melanie. You know that."

"Yes."

She knew that he had to go but hoped that something in his make-up and his feeling for her would cause him to stay. As he reached the door he turned and the tears in her eyes accused him of betrayal. He had to close the door resolutely behind him to shut out her sobs as she collapsed back on the pillow. Had he listened further he too was sure he might have stayed.

The streets were full of running men, townsmen and yardsmen and the Catenor militia gathering together, and overall the sounds of horns calling from somewhere out in the night. Jacobi, having declined to adopt a partisan approach, had no set point of rendezvous and for this he was suddenly glad. He took the quietest alleys leading out of town, then along the road to the yards, setting up a good jog-trot the whole distance. Behind him he could hear carts setting out from Catenor, while, in front, watch-fires were being lighted around the yard perimeters by the yardsmen on duty. At this point he saw no sign of the raiders and had only the horns' evidence that they indeed had come.

At the yard gates he was stopped by a yardsman with a pike and forced back into a circle of firelight for recognition. His vitriolic condemnation of the delay was a performance worthy of Timor himself and a gate was immediately drawn open for him to enter. Inside the yards he had the place to himself and this suited his purpose well. He was halfway through to his destination when heavy fighting broke out near the gas stockade and a burst of flame pointed the pattern of the raiders' approach to the menace of the Catenor yards.

At the foot of the scaffold lay the components of his precious hydrogen ship. Tomorrow it should have proudly risen to shape and then taken flight for all in Catenor to see the progress in shipbuilding. Tonight it was a neat-stacked fold of fabric, rope and canvas above the deck which housed the engine. He knew precisely what he had to do. He pulled the drain plug from the fuel tank and allowed the crude oils to flow out on to the decking. When he was reasonably sure the deck and ropes were saturated he took a burner igniter and some chaff and encouraged a small fire which he threw bodily on to the oil-soaked decking. The resultant flare, which encompassed deck, fabric, rigging and scaffold, gave pause to raider and defender alike. But the hydrogen ship stood no chance of becoming a raiders' prize.

FIVE

CATENOR underestimated the raiders badly. Apparently in temporary collusion with several other pirate parties, over a hundred and fifty ships had landed in the vicinity and it was a toughened, ruthless army which hit Catenor and the yards that night. By morning the fight was nearly over. Using a feint attack on the yards as a diversion, the main spearhead of the raiders' forces had gone straight into Catenor with one specific purpose—hostages. The women and children had been herded like cattle out into the fields and any who opposed had been slain without mercy. Pockets of resistance in the town had been burned down or smoked out and nearly a quarter of Catenor was smoking ruins at the coming of the dawn.

Deceived by this pattern of tactics and embittered by the savagery of the attack, Timor, who held the yards intact save for the gas stockade, refused to surrender his installation. The raiders sent him the limbless torso of a young girl and promised him another every hour until he gave in. Soon ragged white flags flew upon the lookout towers and the raiders had their way. Jacobi stood with arms folded and watched, knowing that he alone would have to win the battle that the rest of Catenor had lost. The message of the mutilated child's body was not lost on him. Guild-rule or no Guild-rule, a Journeyman made partisan by witness to such an atrocity was no mean enemy.

Jacobi foresaw the coming developments even if Timor did not. The Cloudmaster, his face full-thunder, went out to meet the raiding chief and his aides. They knocked him down in the dust and kicked him and passed on into the yards dragging a captive behind them. The captive was Melanie, hands bound and scolding like a fury. They made a rope halter and tethered her to a post like any common beast.

"Where's the Journeyman?"

"Here." Jacobi came forward, arms folded.

"Ah!" The raiders' leader, a bearded giant called Dacon, signalled swift acknowledgment. "You would be Jacobi. We've heard of you." He nodded in the direction of Melanie, straining at her bonds. "In fact we know a great deal about what motivates Catenor. The woman is primary hostage to ensure your cooperation."

"The Guild is not amenable to blackmail," said Jacobi. "Neither does it operate under duress. As a Cloudsman, if you have a reasonable claim to Guild service, you shall receive it. Otherwise you may rot."

"Service? You damned whelp!" Dacon blazed with anger. "It's not service we want from you—it's hydrogen."

"Hydrogen? In those sacks?" Jacobi looked across the fields to where the raiding cloudcraft were scattered across the fields.

"Yes, in those, Journeyman."

"No," said Jacobi flatly. "If you want hydrogen you'd best buy a Journeyman-at-bond from the Guild. There's more to hydrogen flight than filling cloudships."

"Zeus! I could afford three hundred men for the price of one Guild bond. But why should I bother when you will provide it free of charge?"

"The Guild does nothing free of charge. If you want hydrogen you'll pay Guild price."

Jacobi turned and walked deliberately away towards Timor's office. After a dozen paces he was caught and swung roughly round again to face the raiding chief.

"You mistake your position here, Journeyman. Are we to treat you with presents as we did with Timor?"

"No," said Jacobi, "it is you who mistake your position. You can't kill everyone in Catenor, because you're outnumbered by several to one. Only your hostages protect you. But if you continue your atrocities on the hostages they won't constitute protection any more. When that point comes the population will tear you apart with their bare hands if necessary."

Dacon was amused. "It was scarcely our intention to settle here."

"You've some small craft out there," said Jacobi, nodding to the field, "and you've already come a fair way. Don't tell me you've fuel enough for your burners to carry the whole of you right across the plains."

"No," said Dacon, discomfited by the accuracy of Jacobi's summary. "Hence our interest in hydrogen. With it we can dispense with using fuel."

"And save at Guild price you'll get no hydrogen from me."

"I think we shall." Dacon looked towards Melanie. "Yon's a pretty girl and ripe too. I'd imagine you'd hear her screaming a long ways from here if we put our minds to it."

Jacobi faced him squarely. "Try it. See how many women you have to torture or how many children you need to mutilate before you precipitate the bloodbath you cannot possibly hope to win." He spat contemptuously on the cloud-pirate's ankles, then turned his back and walked away, praying the shadows of Guild responsibility would clog his ears with clay and poke the eyes out of his imagination. Every step he took was a determined effort and every muscle movement demanded voluntary control as if, in the interim, he'd forgotten how to walk. He reached the stairs leading to Timor's office and had ascended the first three steps before he dared to turn. Behind him there had been no sound at all.

Dacon had followed and was ten paces off, standing now looking up at Jacobi.

"Very well, Journeyman! What *is* the Guild price for hydrogen?"

"Simply that, when you have it, you leave Catenor immediately. No more killing, no rape, no hostages and no women to be taken."

"Only that?" Dacon's face registered his disbelief. "I don't follow your reasoning, Journeyman. Where's the Guild gain in that?"

"That's the Guild's affair. Do you want to pay more?"

"No. I accept the price. In return for my ships filled with hydrogen I will see it goes as you ask. But we came here for a reason—and that was to destroy Timor's yards. You say nothing of that in your bargain."

Jacobi shrugged. "Leave the hydrogen plant undamaged, but with the rest you may do as you will. It's no concern of mine."

Timor had come back into the yards, his mouth bloody, and, shorn of the aura of control and authority he normally carried about him, he seemed to have aged incredibly. Now he was but an old and beaten man, ignored by the raiders and unable to surmount the circumstances which had befallen him. He found his daughter tethered to a post and tried to interfere, but the pirates merely threatened the girl with a knife and he moved on helplessly. Then he saw Jacobi and Dacon and came hesitantly across the yards to know what they were saying.

He could not have caught the words but must have guessed the gist of the conversation, for suddenly he roared with anger and drew himself back to something of his old stature.

"Jacobi, by the gods, I'll make no bargains with murderers!"

"The bargain is already struck in the Guild's name," said Jacobi.

"Then the Guild will have to fulfil it. You'll get no aid from Catenor."

"I need the crew to make hydrogen."

"Any man of mine who helps you will have a sorry time living in these parts hereafter. And you'll likely find it healthier yourself to leave if you assist this hell-spawn."

"Then get back with the women and children," said Jacobi, "because you've entered your second childhood all too sudden." He turned to Dacon. "Find me men and I'll instruct them what to do. Start bringing your craft here to the yards and have plenty of tethers prepared."

"They'll get no hydrogen here." Timor pushed his way past the pirate and started up the steps towards Jacobi and there was murder in his eyes.

This time it was Jacobi who knocked Timor into the dust.

The word spread fast and support for Timor was unanimous among the men of Catenor. No yardsman would cooperate with the raiders, even under the threat of death, and the raiders finally cleared them from the yards. In the town feeling against Jacobi ran high for his quisling activities, though he had no opportunity to explain the bargain he had struck, nor did he attempt to do so. Melanie was one of the last of Timor's people to leave the yards. They took her, unbound now and silent, back to the rest of the women. Her only action as she passed through the gate was to spit in Jacobi's face and look at him, not in anger, as might have been expected, but with disgust and repugnance, such as one reserves for something unspeakably obscene.

The reasoning behind Jacobi's unpopularity was obvious. Having already some craft with engines, the raiders had a great superiority in flight. With hydrogen also, they would be untouchable. Not only Catenor but the entire province would be permanently wide-open to plunder and rape and no man might raise his hand against the raiders for fear of massive retribution. This, coupled with the loss of Timor's yards, would settle the area back into the fringes of the dark ages of lawless poverty and fear from which it had so painfully striven to emerge.

Despite their loose and lawless association, the raiders were remarkably efficient when there was work to be done. All were expert Cloudsmen and many were ex-yardsmen dispossessed of their jobs by attitude or circumstance. Contrary to his expectation, Jacobi found no difficulty in instructing a raiding crew to work the hydrogen plant and well-organised dray-crews soon had the first ships in position ready for filling. As the first ships received their charge they were weighted with sand and hauled clear of the workings to allow new craft to be brought in.

With some one hundred and fifty balloons to fill, progress was slow and Jacobi initially doubted if the coal stocks would be sufficient. But by continuous operation of the coke-making plant to ensure the most efficient yield, plus the stock of coke he had already accumulated, he managed to find the majority of the gas he needed. Several of the raiders' smaller craft he rejected as unsuitable for filling and these the raiders burned rather than leave them in Catenor.

The whole operation took three days. In that time the hostages had been permitted to slowly filter back into the town without further molestation. The raiders' pickets in the town had been withdrawn in stages and the pirate manpower was now almost entirely concentrated in the yards. The yards themselves were being systematically destroyed: the forges smashed, the fabric and rigging sheds burned, the methane chambers holed and the pumps and pipework bent and broken. Through the devastation Timor wandered daily without hindrance, watching his lifetime's work being reduced to rubble. Occasionally he came near to Jacobi and stood in silent witness, his face completely without expression.

All was complete by late afternoon on the third day. Since control of altitude in the gas-filled cloudships could not easily be attained without loss of hydrogen, Jacobi had suggested that the assorted ships could be kept more closely together by loosely roping the craft in groups. The idea of a cloud-city of associated craft appealed to the raiders and thus it was mainly in three groups of linked ships that the raiders departed on a slow wind. Dacon's and a few of the larger ships were unroped and these remained as a rearguard until the main force was well aloft.

Timor's people and the citizens of Catenor kept well away during the hours of departure, presumably not wishing to incite an incident unnecessarily. But they were black on the fields between Catenor and the yards, watching and waiting. Dacon observed the slowly advancing horde with some amusement. When the raiders went, Jacobi would be left the sole occupant of the remains of what had once been the shipyards of Catenor—and Jacobi was not very popular.

As a final gesture the pirate called Jacobi to his side and nodded to the taut, human tide crossing the fields. "How about it, Journeyman? Do you fancy becoming a cloud-pirate? We could make good use of your talents and you've a hard welcome coming to you when your friends arrive. We've not left them enough solid wood to make a gallows, but doubtless they'll be satisfied with stoning."

"Thanks," said Jacobi, "but I'll take my chances here. I'll wager I'll live long enough to serve out my bond."

Dacon raised an enquiring eyebrow. "Then you've more faith in human nature than I. Farewell, Journeyman, and take care of that hydrogen plant. One day we may have need of more, and then we'll be back."

"I'll ask Timor to be sure to keep it hot for you," said Jacobi. "There's little enough else left for him to do."

With the raiders gone, Jacobi sat on a pile of rubble and watched the departing ships rise to become mere shadows in the clouds, then fade to nothing. Their disappearance was so absolute that they might well never have existed. But the solid witness of their recent tenure was unmistakable. The once proud shipyards of Catenor were now rubble and ash heaps and desolation. Somewhere to the fore was a small grave where the remains of a murdered child had been roughly buried in a shroud, the ends of which still showed above the ground. Around Catenor there would be more graves still. If Jacobi had ever again needed a reminder that the Guild ideal was the only way, then the stark picture about him would long serve to trigger his reactions.

He was aware from the almost silent sounds of entry that the townsfolk and yardsmen had reached the yards and he sensed rather than saw that Timor was at their head. He did not bother to turn and face them because any attempt at explanation from him would have been wasted words. Whatever they intended to do to him they would do regardless. So he sat and listened to their curiously wake-like approach and so was completely unprepared for the hand which fell suddenly on his shoulder.

"Peace, Jacobi!" It was Timor, his eyes on the clouds where the raiders had last been seen. "I think I know what you've done." He sat on the rubble beside the Journeyman. "Promise me not many of them will be alive by morning."

Jacobi turned to look into Timor's old, steel eyes.

"Not more than about three dozen, I expect."

"Aye! And how many of them were here?"

"Nearly six hundred."

"Aye!" said Timor again, considering the enormity of

183

the coming event. "For a non-combatant, Jacobi, you make a terrible enemy. How will they go?"

"After sundown, when the atmosphere cools, they'll lose height," said Jacobi. "Because I forgot to instruct them better some of them will attempt to light their burners. Those ships will either catch fire or explode. Those roped together with them will likely go also."

"And if they should forbear to light their burners?"

"Then every ship has somewhere in its rigging one of my sodium darts. Perhaps tomorrow or the day beyond they'll find rain or cloud moisture sufficient for the purpose. If six of those six hundred are alive later than three days from now it'll be only because the gods have blessed them. Is that revenge enough for you, Cloudmaster?"

"Revenge, aye!" The Cloudmaster looked moodily about the ruined yards. "But not compensation. There'll be hard times in Catenor before we make cloudships here again."

As he spoke there was the sound of muffled thunder from above. Glancing upwards they saw a cloud light up, rose-tinted from within, followed by more thunder. Then away across the fields things fell burning from the sky through the cloud cover. Then whole ships came falling, wreathed in flame, and the black dots of men precipitated into death. There was no telling how many, but for fifteen incredible minutes the display continued and the fields were bright with fires against the growing dusk. Perhaps a third of the raiding armada fell in that time and those which escaped carried the sodium seed of their own death unknowingly somewhere in the rigging. Guild-rule, or no Guild-rule, a Journeyman made partisan by witness to atrocity was no mean enemy.

Despite their grief and their losses, the citizens of Catenor celebrated Jacobi's victory that night. For the first time in memory the threat of raiders had been removed completely from the town. The loss of the yards and the death of some of their kinsfolk saddened the occasion but did not quieten its expression. But this time Jacobi was restrained and unable to lose himself in the revels. The weight of Guild obligation now firmly entrapped his shoulders and its veil of shadows was suffocating about his face. As with Timor, the recent events had aged him greatly, and he was beginning to discern what loads the Guild elders habitually took upon themselves.

He took himself early from the celebrations and sought Timor at his house. The Cloudmaster was resting. His face, under the light from the dim oil lamp, was more lined and more aged than Jacobi ever remembered seeing it before. His old, shrewd eyes, however, had lost none of their steely comprehension.

"It's not a social call that brings you here at this hour, Jacobi."

"No. I want to buy your shipyards for the Guild."

Timor shrugged. "I have no shipyards. Only heaps of rubble."

"All the better. It will save us the work of demolition. The ships we want to build here will have no use for fabric and rigging."

"You speak in riddles," said Timor tiredly. "There are no such ships as those. But anyway, state your terms."

"The Guild will pay fair price for your yards as they stood before the raiders came. A Guild cell will be established here and you will become a Guild elder. All your former staff here will be guaranteed employment and many more besides. Also the Guild will set up schools, libraries, hospitals, factories, and whatever Catenor requires to develop as the industrial and commercial capital of Europe."

Timor considered this in silence for a long time, then: "You bargain in the same way that you fight, Jacobi—without compromise."

"Then it's a bargain?"

"It's a bargain. I'd be a fool to refuse. But in point you buy nothing from me but the knowledge and hand-skills of a few hundred craftsmen."

"That's all I need," said Jacobi. "From that all the rest will follow."

"And if I'm to become an elder of the Guild does that mean I also learn from whence the Guild gets its knowledge?"

"Its administration will be part of your responsibility," said Jacobi. "The ancients had machines they called computers which could read and be aware of what they read. They crystallised vast libraries down to strips of film and reels of tape and gave the computers access to these stores of information. A man could ask for all that was ever known of a subject and the machines would give it to him. Then, when the last dark-age began, the ancients sealed down their equipments and left them for us."

"So this is the oracle from which the Guild gets its knowledge?"

"Something more tangible than an oracle, but it works as well. Journeymen are educated from birth in Guild schools where the level of knowledge taught from computer information is roughly two centuries ahead of the times in which we live."

"Then the purpose of the Guild is not to advance the art of building cloudcraft, but simply to spread this knowledge?"

"Just that," said Jacobi. "But to spread it in such a way that its introduction doesn't cause more misery than it relieves. Knowledge is power and we have no wish to create powerful tyrants through our own efforts."

"But why pretend to concentrate on cloudcraft?"

"It's a good cover and it presents an advancing technology that automatically scatters about it a lot of other skills and trades. In this way can the Guild re-fashion whole communities without anyone even suspecting the cause of the transformation."

"I suspected," said Timor quietly. "That's why Catenor waited three whole years for Jacobi. You see, I insisted on having nothing but the best."

Leaving Timor's house, Jacobi turned by a long route across the fields around the town, half fearing to put into action the next move because of the years of involvement which it would bring upon him. Along the dark ways, with only occasional moonlight to guide him, he chanced upon courting couples neglecting the rejoicing in the town for more deep and personal approaches. Momentarily he wished that Melanie was by his side, but he stamped the regret angrily from his mind, knowing that dreams separated by two centuries of technical education can never quite be reconciled.

Looking outward, he began to make his plans. The old shipyards, together with the farm adjoining, would make a landing strip—grass at first, and start with biplanes. Later—much later—concrete runways for the jets. Thus would a new breed of cloudcraft rise out of Catenor. And one day, perhaps, even spacecraft . . .

His steps took him back to the attic. It seemed now as empty and impersonal as his life. Melanie had no use for either since the night the raiders came. The message store of his communicator issued a single interrogatory symbol, indicating that the device had been contacted in his absence and a reply was awaited. Jacobi thought for a moment, then opened the keyboard in the top and typed his message slowly, noticing his hands were shaking.

JACOBI—CATENOR—TO TIRC YORKTOWN NEW YORK
VIA LA GAUDE AND SATELLITE LINK—MESSAGE

BEGINS QUOTE CATENOR YARDS DESTROYED BY RAIDERS—TOWN AND POPULATION SUBSTANTIALLY INTACT—RAIDERS DESTROYED—INSIST IMMEDIATE UPGRADING CATENOR TO PHASE FIVE LEVEL IMPERATIVE ELSE YOU LOSE EUROPE UNQUOTE— JACOBI—CATENOR

The reaction was immediate. Before he could take his fingers from the keyboard the print-out began to spill words as if in a frenzy.

TIRC NEW YORK TO JACOBI URGENT—GOOD DECISION IF YOU CAN HANDLE IT—GUILD ALREADY APPROVED PHASE FIVE IN CATENOR—MASSIVE AID WILL BE ROUTED TO YOU VIA HELIUM DIRIGIBLES—ALL EUROPEAN OPERATIONS NOW CENTRED ON CATENOR UNDER YOUR CONTROL—GOOD LUCK—HOW DOES IT FEEL TO BE RUNNING YOUR OWN CIVILISATION QUERY—

Jacobi's fingers returned to the keyboard, and after establishing contact codes he typed one further word in answer:
—HELL—

SAINTE-BEUVE